Ready To Were

Shift Happens Series Book One

By

Robyn Peterman

What others are saying about this book

Acknowledgements

I have wanted to write about shifters for a long time. It took my buddy Kathleen Brooks inviting me into an anthology to get my butt in gear! Thank you Kathleen for pulling me in and giving me the inspiration to write this book! You rock!

As always I would be nowhere without Donna McDonald, JM Madden and Kris Calvert! Thank you. Candace and Christi, you ladies rock! And Mary Yakovets and my mom saved me from some hideous grammar mistakes! Love you. Lastly Rebecca Poole, you are a cover goddess!

Smooches to all.

Dedication

For Steve—I will love you till the end of time.

Chapter 1

"You're joking."

"No, actually I'm not," my boss said and slapped the folder into my hands. "You leave tomorrow morning and I don't want to see your hairy ass till this is solved."

I looked wildly around her office for something to lob at her head. It occurred to me that might not be the best of ideas, but desperate times led to stupid measures. She could not do this to me. I'd worked too hard and I wasn't going back. Ever.

"First of all, my ass is not hairy except on a full moon and you're smoking crack if you think I'm going back to Georgia."

Angela crossed her arms over her ample chest and narrowed her eyes at me. "Am I your boss?" she asked.

"Is this a trick question?"

She huffed out an exasperated sigh and ran her hands through her spiked 'do making her look like she'd been electrocuted. "Essie, I am cognizant of how you feel about Hung Island, Georgia, but there's a disaster of major proportions on the horizon and I have no choice."

"Where are you sending Clark and Jones?" I demanded.

"New York and Miami."

"Oh my god," I shrieked. "Who did I screw over in a former life that those douches get to go to cool cities and I have to go home to an island called Hung?"

"Those douches *do* have hairy asses and not just on a full moon. You're the only female agent I have that looks like a model so you're going to Georgia. Period."

"Fine. I'll quit. I'll open a bakery."

Angela smiled and an icky feeling skittered down my spine. "Excellent, I'll let you tell the Council that all the money they invested in your training is going to be flushed down the toilet because you want to bake cookies."

The Council consisted of supernaturals from all sorts of species. The branch that currently had me by the metaphorical balls was WTF—Werewolf Treaty Federation. They were the worst as far as stringent rules and consequences went. The Vampyres were loosey goosey, the Witches were nuts and the freakin' Fairies were downright pushovers, but not the Weres. Nope, if you enlisted you were in for life. It had sounded so good when the insanely sexy recruiting officer had come to our local Care For Your Inner Were meeting.

Training with the best of the best. Great salary with benefits. Apartment and company car. But the kicker for me was that it was fifteen hours away from the hell I grew up in. No longer was I Essie from Hung Island, Georgia— *and who in their right mind would name an island Hung*—I was Agent Essie McGee of the Chicago WTF. The irony of the initials was a source of pain to most Werewolves, but went right over the Council's heads due to the simple fact that they were older than dirt and oblivious to pop culture.

Yes, I'd been disciplined occasionally for mouthing off to superiors and using the company credit card for shoes, but other than that I was a damn good agent. I'd graduated at the top of my class and was the go-to girl for messy and dangerous assignments that no one in their right mind would take... I'd singlehandedly brought down three rogue Weres who were selling secrets to the Dragons— another supernatural species. The Dragons shunned the Council, had their own little club and a psychotic desire to rule the world. Several times they'd come close due to the fact that they were loaded and Weres from the New Jersey Pack were easily bribed. Not to mention the fire-breathing thing...

I was an independent woman living in the Windy City. I had a gym membership, season tickets to the Cubs and a gay Vampyre best friend named Dwayne. What more did a girl need?

Well, possibly sex, but the *bastard* had ruined me for other men...

Hank "The Tank" Wilson was the main reason I'd rather chew my own paw off than go back to Hung Island, Georgia. Six foot three of obnoxious, egotistical, perfect-assed, alpha male Werewolf. As the alpha of my local Pack he had decided it was high time I got mated...to him. I, on the other hand, had plans—big ones and they didn't include being barefoot and pregnant at the beck and call of a player.

So I did what any sane, rational woman would do. I left in the middle of the night with a suitcase, a flyer from the hot recruiter and enough money for a one-way bus ticket to freedom. Of course, nothing ever turns out as planned... The apartment was the size of a shoe box, the car was used and smelled like French fries and the benefits didn't kick in till I turned one hundred and twenty five. We Werewolves had long lives.

"Angela, you really can't do this to me." Should I get down on my knees? I was so desperate I wasn't above begging.

"Why? What happened there, Essie? Were you in some kind of trouble I should know about?" Her eyes narrowed, but she wasn't yelling.

I think she liked me...kind of. The way a mother would like an annoying spastic two year old who belonged to someone else.

"No, not exactly," I hedged. "It's just that..."

"Weres are disappearing and presumed dead. Considering no one knows of our existence besides other supernaturals, we have a problem. Furthermore, it seems like humans might be involved."

My stomach lurched and I grabbed Angela's office chair for balance. "Locals are missing?" I choked out. My grandma Bobby Sue was still there, but I'd heard from her last night. She'd harangued me about getting my belly button pierced. Why I'd put that on Instagram was beyond me. I was gonna hear about that one for the next eighty years or so.

"Not just missing—more than likely dead. Check the folder," Angela said and poured me a shot of whiskey.

With trembling hands I opened the folder. This had to be a joke. I felt ill. I'd gone to high school with Frankie Mac and Jenny Packer. Jenny was as cute as a button and was the cashier at the Piggly Wiggly. Frankie Mac had been the head cheerleader and cheated on every test since the fourth grade. Oh my god, Debbie Swink? Debbie Swink had been voted most likely to succeed and could do a double backwards flip off the high dive. She'd busted her head open countless times before she'd perfected it. Her mom was sure she'd go to the Olympics.

"I know these girls," I whispered.

"Knew. You knew them. They all were taking classes at the modeling agency."

"What modeling agency? There's no modeling agency on Hung Island." I sifted through the rest of the folder with a knot the size of a cantaloupe in my stomach. More names and faces I recognized. Sandy Moongie? *Wait a minute.*

"Um, not to speak ill of the dead, but Sandy Moongie was the size of a barn…she was modeling?"

"Worked the reception desk." Angela shook her head and dropped down on the couch.

"This doesn't seem that complicated. It's fairly black and white. Whoever is running the modeling agency is the perp."

"The modeling agency is Council sponsored."

I digested that nugget in silence for a moment.

"And the Council is running a modeling agency, why?"

"Word is that we're heading toward revealing ourselves to the humans and they're trying to find the most attractive representatives to do so."

"That's a joke, right?" *What kind of dumb ass plan was that?*

"I wish it was." Angela picked up my drink and downed it. "I'm getting too old for this shit," she muttered as she refilled the shot glass, thought better of it and just swigged from the bottle.

"Is the Council aware that I'm going in?"

"What do you think?"

"I think they're old and stupid and that they send in dispensable agents like me to clean up their shitshows," I grumbled.

"Smart girl."

"Who else knows about this? Clark? Jones?"

"They know," she said wearily. "They're checking out agencies in New York and Miami."

"Isn't it conflict of interest to send me where I know everyone?"

"It is, but you'll be able to infiltrate and get in faster that way. Besides, no one has disappeared from the other agencies yet."

There was one piece I still didn't understand. "How are humans involved?"

She sighed and her head dropped back onto her broad shoulders. "Humans are running the agency."

It took a lot to render me silent, like learning my grandma had been a stripper in her youth, and that all male Werewolves were hung like horses... but this was horrific.

"Who in the hell thought that was a good idea? My god, half the female Weres I know sprout tails when flash bulbs go off. We won't have to come out, they can just run billboards of hot girls with hairy appendages coming out of their asses."

"It's all part of the *Grand Plan*. If the humans see how wonderful and attractive we are, the issue of knowingly living alongside of us will be moot."

Again. Speechless.

"When are Council elections?" It was time to vote some of those turd knockers out.

"Essie." Angela rolled her eyes and took another swig. "There are no elections. They're appointed and serve for life."

"I knew that," I mumbled. Skipping Were History class was coming back to bite me in the butt.

"I'll go." There was no way I couldn't. Even though my knowledge of the hierarchy of my race was fuzzy, my skills were top notch and trouble seemed to find me. In any other job that would suck, but in mine, it was an asset.

"Good. You'll be working with the local Pack alpha. He's also the sheriff there. Name's Hank Wilson. You know him?"

"Yep." *Biblically. I knew the son of a bitch biblically.*

***

"You're gonna bang him."

"I am not gonna bang him."

"You are so gonna bang him."

"Dwayne, if I hear you say that I'm gonna bang him one more time, I will not let you borrow my black Mary Jane pumps. Ever again."

Dwayne made the international "zip the lip and throw away the key" sign while silently mouthing that I was going to bang Hank.

"I think you should bang him if he's a hot as you said." Dwayne made himself comfortable on my couch and turned on the TV.

"When did I ever say he was hot?" I demanded as I took the remote out of his hands. I was not watching any more *Dance Moms.* "I never said he was hot."

"Paaaaleese," Dwayne flicked his pale hand over his shoulder and rolled his eyes.

"What was that?"

"What was what?" he asked, confused.

"That shoulder thing you just did."

"Oh, I was flicking my hair over my shoulder in a *girlfriend* move."

"Okay, don't do that. It doesn't work. You're as bald as a cue ball."

"But it's the new move," he whined.

Oh my god, Vampyres were such high maintenance. "According to who?" I yanked my suitcase out from under my bed and started throwing stuff in.

"Kim Kardashian."

I refused to dignify that with so much as a look.

"Fine," he huffed. "But if you say one word about my skinny jeans I am so out of here."

I considered it, but I knew he was serious. As crazy as he drove me, I adored him. He was my only real friend in Chicago and I had no intention of losing him.

"I know he's hot," Dwayne said. "Look at you—you're so gorge it's redonkulous. You're all legs and boobs and hair and lips—you're far too beautiful to be hung up on a goober."

"Are you calling me shallow?" I snapped as I ransacked my tiny apartment for clean clothes. Damn it, tomorrow was laundry day. I was going to have to pack dirty clothes.

"So he's ugly and puny and wears bikini panties?"

"No! He's hotter than Satan's underpants and he wears boxer briefs," I shouted. "You happy?"

"He's actually a nice guy."

"You've met Hank?" I was so confused I was this close to making fun of his skinny jeans just so he would leave.

"Satan. He's not as bad as everyone thinks."

How was it that everyone I came in contact with today stole my ability to speak? Thankfully, I was interrupted by a knock at my door.

"You expecting someone?" Dwayne asked as he pilfered the remote back and found *Dance Moms*.

"No."

I peeked through the peephole. Nobody came to my place except Dwayne and the occasional pizza delivery guy or Chinese food take out guy or Indian food take out guy. *Wait. What the hell was my boss doing here?*

"Angela?"

"You going to let me in?"

"Depends."

"Open the damn door."

I did.

Angela tromped into my shoebox and made herself at home. Her hair was truly spectacular. It looked like she might have even pulled out a clump on the left side. "You want to tell me why the sheriff and alpha of Hung Island, Georgia says he won't work with you?"

13

"Um…no?"

"He said he had a hard time believing someone as flaky and irresponsible as you had become an agent for the Council and he wants someone else." Angela narrowed her eyes at me and took the remote form Dwayne. "Spill it, Essie."

I figured the best way to handle this was to lie— hugely. However, gay Vampyre boyfriends had a way of interrupting and screwing up all your plans.

"Well, you see…"

"He's her mate and he dipped his stick in several other…actually *many* other oil tanks. So she dumped his furry player ass, snuck away in the middle of the night and hadn't really planned on ever going back there again." Dwayne sucked in a huge breath, which was ridiculous because Vampyres didn't breathe.

It took everything I had not to scream and go all Wolfy. "Dwayne, clearly you want me to go medieval on your lily white ass because I can't imagine why you would utter such bullshit to my boss."

"Doesn't sound like bullshit to me," Angela said as she channel surfed and landed happily on an old episode of *Cagney and Lacey*. "We might have a problem here."

"Are you replacing me?" Hank Wilson had screwed me over once when I was his. He was not going to do it again when I wasn't.

"Your call," she said. Dwayne, who was an outstanding shoplifter, covertly took back the remote and flipped over to the Food Channel. Angela glanced up at the tube and gave Dwayne the evil eye.

"I refuse to watch lesbians fight crime in the eighties. I'll get hives," he explained, tilted his head to the right and gave Angela a smile. He was so pretty it was silly— piercing blue eyes and body to die for. Even my boss had a hard time resisting his charm.

"Fine," she grumbled.

"Excuse me," I yelled. "This conversation is about me, not testosterone ridden women cops with bad hair, hives or food. It's my life we're talking about here—me, me, me!" My voice had risen to decibels meant to attract stray animals within a ten-mile radius, evidenced by the wincing and ear covering.

"Essie, are you done?" Dwayne asked fearfully.

"Possibly. What did you tell him?" I asked Angela.

"I told him the Council has the last word in all matters. Always. And if he had a problem with it, he could take it up with the elders next month when they stay awake long enough to listen to the petitions of their people."

"Oh my god, that's awesome," I squealed. "What did he say?"

"That if we send you down, he'll give you bus money so you can hightail your sorry cowardly butt right back out of town."

Was she grinning at me, and was that little shit Dwayne jotting the conversation down in the notes section on his phone?

"Let me tell you something," I ground out between clenched teeth as I confiscated Dwayne's phone and pocketed it. "I am going to Hung Island, Georgia tomorrow and I will kick his ass. I will find the killer first and then I will castrate the alpha of the Georgia Pack...with a dull butter knife."

Angela laughed and Dwayne jackknifed over on the couch in a visceral reaction to my plan. I stomped into my bathroom and slammed the door to make my point, then pressed my ear to the rickety wood to hear them talk behind my back.

"I'll bet you five hundred dollars she's gonna bang him," Dwayne told Angela.

"I'll bet you a thousand that you're right," she shot back.

"You're on."

Chapter 2

"This music is going to make me yack." Dwayne moaned and put his hands over his ears.

Trying to ignore him wasn't working. I promised myself I wouldn't put him out of the car until we were at least a hundred miles outside of Chicago. I figured anything less than that wouldn't be the kind of walk home that would teach him a lesson.

"First of all, Vampyres can't yack and I don't recall asking you to come with me," I replied and cranked up The Clash.

"You have got to be kidding." He huffed and flipped the station to Top Forty. "You need me."

"Really?"

"Oh my god," Dwayne shrieked. "I luurrve Lady Gaga."

"That's why I need you?"

"Wait. What?"

"I need you because you love The Gaga?"

Dwayne rolled his eyes. "Everyone loves The Gaga. You need me because you need to show your hometown and Hank the Hooker that you have a new man in your life."

"You're a Vampyre."

"Yes, and?"

"Well, um…you're gay."

"What does that have to do with anything? I am hotter than asphalt in August and I have a huge package."

While his points were accurate, there was no mistaking his sexual preference. The skinny jeans, starched muscle shirt, canvas Mary Janes and the gold hoop earrings were an undead giveaway.

"You know, I think you should just be my best friend. I want to show them I don't need a man to make it in this world...okay?" I glanced over and he was crying. Shitshitshit. Why did I always say the wrong thing? "Dwayne, I'm sorry. You can totally be my..."

"You really consider me your best friend?" he blubbered. "I have never had a best friend in all my three hundred years. I've tried, but I just..." He broke down and let her rip.

"Yes, you're my best friend, you idiot. Stop crying. Now." Snark I could deal with. Tears? Not so much.

"Oh my god, I just feel so happy," he gushed. "And I want you to know if you change your mind about the boyfriend thing just wink at me four times and I'll stick my tongue down your throat."

"Thanks, I'll keep that in mind."

"Anything for my best friend. Ohhh Essie, are there any gay bars in Hung?"

This was going to be a wonderful trip.

***

One way in to Hung Island, Georgia. One way out. The bridge was long and the ocean was beautiful. Sun glistened off the water and sparkled like diamonds. Dwayne was quiet for the first time in fifteen hours. As we pulled into town, my gut clenched and I started to sweat. This was stupid—so very stupid. The nostalgic pull of this place was huge and I felt sucked back in immediately.

"Holy Hell," Dwayne whispered. "It's beautiful here. How did you leave this place?"

He was right. It was beautiful. It had the small town feel mixed up with the ocean and land full of wild grasses and rolling hills. How did I leave?

"I left because I hate it here," I lied. "We'll do the job, castrate the alpha with a butter knife and get out. You got it?"

"Whatever you say, best friend. Whatever you say." He grinned.

"I'm gonna drop you off at my Grandma Bobby Sue's. She doesn't exactly know we're coming so you have to be on your best behavior."

"Will you be?"

"Will I be what?" God, Vamps were tiresome.

"On your best behavior."

"Absolutely not. We're here."

I stopped my crappy car in front of a charming old Craftsman. Flowers covered every inch of the yard. It was a literal explosion of riotous color and I loved it. Granny hated grass—found the color offensive. It was the home I grew up in. Granny BS, as everyone loved to call her, had raised me after my parents died in a horrific car accident when I was four. I barely remembered my parents, but Granny had told me beautiful bedtime stories about them my entire childhood.

"OMG, this place is so cute I could scream." Dwayne squealed and jumped out of the car into the blazing sunlight. All the stories about Vamps burning to ash or sparkling like diamonds in the sun were a myth. The only thing that could kill Weres and Vamps were silver bullets, decapitation, fire and a silver stake in the heart.

Grabbing Dwayne by the neck of his muscle shirt, I stopped him before he went tearing into the house. "Granny is old school. She thinks Vamps are...you know."

"Blood sucking leeches who should be eliminated?" Dwayne grinned from ear to ear. He loved a challenge. Crap.

"I wouldn't go that far, but she's old and set in her geezer ways. So if you have to, steer clear."

"I'll have her eating kibble out of my manicured lily white hand in no time at...holy shit!" Dwayne screamed and ducked as a blur of Granny BS came flying out of the house and tackled my ass in a bed of posies.

"Mother Humper." I grunted and struggled as I tried to shove all ninety-five pounds of pissed off Grandma Werewolf away from me.

"Gimme that stomach," she hissed as she yanked up my shirt. Thank the Lord I was wearing a bra. Dwayne stood in mute shock and just watched me get my butt handed to me by my tiny granny, who even at eighty was the spitting image of a miniature Sophia Loren in her younger years.

"Get off of me, you crazy old bag," I ground out and tried to nail her with a solid left. She ducked and backslapped my head.

"I said no tattoos and no piercings till you're fifty," she yelled. "Where is it?"

"Oh my GOD," I screeched as I trapped her head with my legs in a scissors hold. "You need meds."

"Tried 'em. They didn't work," she grumbled as she escaped from my hold. She grabbed me from behind as I tried to make a run for my car and ripped out my belly button ring.

"Ahhhhhhhgrhupcraaap, that hurt, you nasty old bat from Hell." I screamed and looked down at the bloody hole that used to be really cute and sparkly. "That was a one carat diamond, you ancient witch."

Both of her eyebrows shot up and I swear to god they touched her hairline.

"Okay, fine," I muttered. "It was cubic zirconia, but it was NOT cheap."

"Hookers have belly rings," she snapped.

"No, hookers have pimps. Normal people have belly rings, or at least they used to," I shot back as I examined the wound that was already closing up.

"Come give your granny a hug," she said and put her arms out.

I approached warily just in case she needed to dole out more punishment for my piercing transgression. She folded me into her arms and hugged me hard. That was the thing about my granny. What you saw was what you got. Everyone always knew where they stood with her. She was mad and then she was done. Period.

"Lawdy, I have missed you, child," she cooed.

"Missed you too, you old cow." I grinned and hugged her back. I caught Dwayne out of the corner of my eye. He was even paler than normal if that was possible and he had placed his hands over his pierced ears.

"Granny, I brought my..."

"Gay Vampyre best friend," she finished my introduction. She marched over to him, slapped her hands on her skinny hips and stared. She was easily a foot shorter than Dwayne, but he trembled like a baby. "Do you knit?" she asked him.

"Um...no, but I've always wanted to learn," he choked out.

She looked him up and down for a loooong minute, grunted and nodded her head. "We'll get along just fine then. Get your asses inside before the neighbors call the cops."

"Why would they call the cops?" Dwayne asked, still terrified.

"Well boy, I live amongst humans and I just walloped my granddaughter on the front lawn. Most people don't think that's exactly normal."

"Point," he agreed and hightailed it to the house.

"Besides," she cackled. "Wouldn't want the sheriff coming over to arrest you now, would we?"

I rolled my eyes and flipped her the bird behind her back.

"Saw that, girlie," she said.

Holy Hell, she still had eyes in the back of her head. If I was smart, I'd grab Dwayne, get in my car and head back to Chicago...but I had a killer to catch and a whole lot to prove here. Smart wasn't on my agenda today.

Chapter 3

The house was exactly the same as it was the last time I saw it a year ago. Granny had more crap on her tables, walls and shelves than an antique store. Dwayne was positively speechless and that was good. Granny took her décor seriously.

"I'm a little disappointed that you want to be a model, Essie," Granny sighed. "You have brains and a mean right hook. Never thought you'd try to coast by with your looks."

I gave Dwayne the *I'll kill you if you tell her I'm an agent on a mission* look and thankfully he understood. While I hated that my granny thought I was shallow and jobless, it was far safer that she didn't know why I was really here.

"Well, you know…I just need to make a few bucks, then get back to my life in the big city," I mumbled. I was a sucky liar around my granny and she knew it.

"Hmmm," she said, staring daggers at me.

"What?" I asked, not exactly making eye contact.

"Nothin'. I'm just lookin'," she challenged.

"And what are you looking at?" I blew out an exasperated sigh and met her eyes. A challenge was a challenge and I *was* a Werewolf…

"A bald face little fibber girl," she crowed. "Spill it or I'll whoop your butt again."

Dwayne quickly backed himself into a corner and slid his phone out of his pocket. That shit was going to video my ass kicking. I had several choices here...destroy Dwayne's phone, elaborate on my lie or come clean. The only good option was the phone.

"Fine," I snapped and sucked in a huge breath. The truth will set you free or result in a trip to the ER... "I'm an agent with the Council—a trained killer for WTF and I'm good at it. The fact that I'm a magnet for trouble has finally paid off. I'm down here to find out who in the hell is killing Werewolves before it blows up in our faces. I plan to find the perps and destroy them with my own hands or a gun, whichever will be most painful. Then I'm going to castrate Hank with a dull butter knife. I plan on a short vacation when I'm done before going back to Chicago."

For the first time in my twenty-eight years on Earth, Granny was mute. It was all kinds of awesome.

"Can I come on the vacation?" Dwayne asked.

"Yes. Cat got your tongue, old woman?" I asked.

"Well, I'll be damned," she said almost inaudibly. "I suppose this shouldn't surprise me. You are a female alpha bitch."

"No," I corrected her. "I'm a lone wolf who wants nothing to do with Pack politics. Ever."

Granny sat her skinny bottom down on her plastic slipcovered floral couch and shook her head. "Ever is a long time, little girl. Well, I suppose I should tell you something now," she said gravely and worried her bottom lip.

"Oh my god, are you sick?" I gasped. Introspective thought was way out of my granny's normal behavior pattern. My stomach roiled. She was all I had left in the world and as much as I wanted to skin her alive, I loved her even more.

"Weres don't get sick. It's about your mamma and daddy. Sit down. And Dwayne, hand over your phone. If I find out you have loose lips, I'll remove them," she told my bestie.

I sat. Dwayne handed. I had thought I knew everything there was to know about my parents, but clearly I was mistaken. Hugely mistaken.

"You remember when I told you your mamma and daddy died in a car accident?"

"Yes," I replied slowly. "You showed me the newspaper articles."

"That's right." She nodded. "They did die in a car, but it wasn't no accident."

Movement was necessary or I thought I might throw up. I paced the room and tried to untangle my thoughts. It wasn't like I'd even known my parents, but they were mine and now I felt cheated somehow. I wanted to crawl out of my skin. My heart pounded so loudly in my chest I was sure the neighbors could hear it. My parents were murdered and this was the first time I was hearing about it?

"Again. Say that again." Surely I'd misunderstood. I'd always been one to jump to conclusions my entire life, but the look on Granny's face told me that this wasn't one of those times.

"They didn't own a hardware store. Well, actually I think they did, but it was just a cover."

"For what?" I asked, fairly sure I knew where this was going.

"They were WTF agents, child, and they were taken out," she said and wrapped her skinny little arms around herself. "Broke my heart—still does."

"And you never told me this? Why?" I demanded and got right up in her face.

"I don't rightly know," she said quietly. "I wanted you to grow up happy and not feel the need for revenge."

She stroked my cheek the way she did when I was a child and I leaned into her hand for comfort. I was angry, but she did what she thought was right. Needless to say, she wasn't right, but...

"Wait, why would I have felt the need for revenge?" I asked. Something was missing.

"The Council was never able to find out who did it, and after a while they gave up."

Everything about that statement was so wrong I didn't know how to react. They gave up? What the hell was that? The Council never gave up. I was trained to get to the bottom of everything. Always.

"That's the most absurd thing I've ever heard. The Council always gets their answers."

Granny shrugged her thin shoulders and rearranged the knickknacks on her coffee table. Wait. Did the Council know more about me than I did? Did my boss Angela know more of my history than I'd ever known?

"I knew that recruiter they sent down here," Granny muttered. "I told him to stay away from you. Told him the Council already took my daughter and son-in-law and they couldn't have you."

"He didn't pay me any more attention than he did anyone else," I told her.

"What did the flyer say that he gave you?"

"Same as everybody's—salary, training, benefits, car, apartment."

"Damn it to hell," she shouted. "No one else's flyer said that. I confiscated them all after the bastard left. I couldn't get to yours cause you were shacking up with the sheriff."

"You lived with Hank the Hooker?" Dwayne gasped. "I thought you just dated a little."

"Hell to the no," Granny corrected Dwayne. "She was engaged. Left the alpha of the Georgia Pack high and dry."

"Enough," I snapped. "Ancient history. I'm more concerned about what kind of cow patty I've stepped in with the Council. The *sheriff* knows why I left. Maybe the Council accepted me cause I can shoot stuff and I have no fear and they have to hire a certain quota of women and..."

"And they want to make sure you don't dig into the past," Dwayne added unhelpfully.

"You're a smart bloodsucker," Granny chimed in.

"Thank you."

"You think the Council had something to do with it," I said. This screwed with my chi almost as much as the Hank situation from a year ago. I had finally done something on my own and it might turn out I hadn't earned any of it.

"I'm not sayin' nothing like that," Granny admonished harshly. "And neither should you. You could get killed."

She was partially correct, but I was the one they sent to kill people who broke Council laws. However, speaking against the Council wasn't breaking the law. The living room had grown too small for my need to move and I prowled the rest of the house with Granny and Dwayne on my heels. I stopped short and gaped at my empty bedroom.

"Where in the hell is my furniture?"

"You moved all your stuff to Hank's and he won't give it back," Granny informed me.

An intense thrill shot through my body, but I tamped it down immediately. I was done with him and he was surely done with me. No one humiliated an alpha and got a second chance. Besides, I didn't want one... Dwayne's snicker earned him a glare that made him hide behind Granny in fear.

"Did you even try to get my stuff back?" I demanded.

"Of course I did," she huffed. "That was your mamma's set from when she was a child. I expected you'd use it for your own daughter someday."

My mamma...My beautiful mamma who'd been murdered along with my daddy. The possibility that the Council had been involved was gnawing at my insides in a bad way.

"I have to compartmentalize this for a minute or at least a couple of weeks," I said as I stood in the middle of my empty bedroom. "I have to do what I was sent here for. But when I'm done, I'll get answers and vengeance."

"Does that mean no vacation?" Dwayne asked.

I stared at Dwayne like he'd grown three heads. He was getting terribly good at rendering me mute.

"That was a good question, Dwayne." Granny patted him on the head like a dog and he preened. "Essie, your mamma and daddy would want you to have a vacation before you get killed finding out what happened to them."

"Can we go to Jamaica?" Dwayne asked.

"Ohhh, I've never been to Jamaica," Granny volunteered.

They were both batshit crazy, but Jamaica did sound kind of nice...

"Fine, but you're paying," I told Dwayne. He was richer than Midas. He'd made outstanding investments in his three hundred years.

"Yayayayayayay!" he squealed.

"I'll call the travel agent," Granny said. "How long do you need to get the bad guy?"

"A week. Give me a week."

Chapter 4

"Well, great balls of fire ain't you a sight for sore eyes!" Junior shouted, came out from behind his desk and trapped me in a hug that made breathing difficult. "Damn girl, if you ain't prettier! What do they put in the water up there in Chicago?"

Junior, aka Jacob *only to his mother*, was the Deputy Sheriff of Hung Island and the Beta of our Pack. He was also Hank's older brother. Hence, I wasn't sure what my reception would be. If the jaws-of-life hug was anything to go by, everything would be just fine. Junior actually should have become Alpha when his dad retired, but he was just a lazy good ol' boy, so the honor went to his younger brother Hank the Cheater.

Junior was every bit as good looking as his brother, but he never did it for me. However, he apparently did it for most of the women within a fifty mile radius.

"I tell you what," he drawled. "I am happy to see you. My baby brother has been in a mood since you left."

"He's been in a mood for a year?" I snorted in disbelief and again tamped down the excited butterflies in my stomach. "I was sure he'd moved on by now."

"Gimme a break, sugar. He's got it so bad for you, it ain't funny."

"Well, he sure had a funny way of showing it," I muttered. Confusion didn't even begin to cover what I was feeling.

"That's interesting," a deep, sexier than hell voice added from behind me. "I could say the same about you."

The air in the room shifted and the seductive power of his voice made me weak. Everything in my body tensed and stood at attention, including my traitorous nipples. Thank god my bra had a little padding—although the padding was useless. Weres could tell everything by scent and there was very little mistaking the cinnamon-laced scent of lust wafting through the room. His and mine. Crap.

Holding my breath, I turned around to face my foe and had to grab onto Junior for purchase so my butt didn't hit the floor...forget about my jaw. Damn it, why could Hank have gotten bald, fat and ugly? He was more beautiful than I remembered. Six foot four of absolute perfection. Dark brown just a little bit too long hair, full lips, cheekbones that could cut glass and an ass that could stop traffic. The only consolation I had was his sharp intake of breath and the way his eyes turned from crystal green to icy blue. That was what happened to wolves when they couldn't mask their desire.

I quickly lowered my eyes, not out of respect. I simply prayed my hazel green eyes hadn't turned blue in response.

"My office. Now," he snapped. "Junior, hold my calls and don't step foot in my office unless you hear gunshots. You understand?"

"You got it, little bro-bro." Junior was grinning from ear to ear and gave me a shove toward Hank's office. I discreetly made sure my gun was still strapped to my inner thigh. I'd worn a sundress to conceal my weapon, *not* because I knew Hank loved them. Wait. Was he planning on shooting me? He so had another thing coming if he tried.

I made my way into the familiar office and bit back every nasty thing I wanted to say. As the door shut behind me I casually took a seat in front of the massive desk we'd had sex on countless times. Crapcrapcrap. Being alone with him was a very bad idea. Where the hell was my self-respect? I did not need a man who wanted me and half the town. I was better than that.

"You've got some explaining to do." He sat down behind his desk in the chair we'd nicknamed the BJ Mobile and crossed his stupidly muscled arms over his stupidly muscled chest.

"No," I said as I regained my confidence and professionalism that had deserted me in the lobby. "I don't. You need to get me up to speed on the case and I need to do what I've been trained to do. Period."

He watched me through narrowed eyes and his jaw worked angrily. Whatever. He had huge balls to think I had explaining to do.

"You left in the middle of the damn night. It took me a week of harassing your granny and massive detective work to find you."

"You knew where I was?" I was shocked. I figured he was so pissed and horny for all the other gals he'd been seeing he'd have been happy I left.

"I know where you live, your patterns, your friends, your grocery, your place of business and where you order takeout from."

"Oookay, that's just creepy." I rolled my eyes and wondered who he'd sent to watch me. It couldn't have been Junior. I would have busted his butt in a minute flat. "Who'd you have on me?"

"I was on you, princess. And when I wasn't, I had a chatty friend who was all too willing to talk about you till the cows came home." He smiled and I wanted to slap the dimple off of his left cheek.

"You paid someone to watch me?" I shouted. I refused to acknowledge that he'd been in Chicago spying on me. *And why in the hell did that turn me on?*

"Nope. Didn't have to."

"That makes no sense whatsoever," I snapped. "No one would watch someone for free."

"If they didn't know they were watching you they would."

"When did you go all James Bond?"

"A man does what a man has to do," he replied.

"Yeah, well most men don't become the town vacuum cleaner," I shot back and then slapped my hand over my mouth. Damn it, I wasn't going to go there.

"What the hell does that mean?" He stood up and was in front of me in a flash.

His scent was making me dizzy and I had the worst urge to jump him, but I gripped the arms of the chair like a vise and maintained my dignity by a thread.

"Nothing. Ancient history. Now that we've reminisced, we need to get down to business," I said coldly, met his gaze and refused to back down.

"Fine. You win round one. On to round two," he said easily—way too easily. "I don't want you here. I don't want you on this case."

"Tough. I am more than capable and you don't have any say, buster boy."

"You did not just call me buster boy."

I bit back my grin and nodded my head. "I did. Now, do you have files for me?"

"Ester..." he said in *that* tone. Fine. We were going there? I hated my name and he knew it, but two could play that game...

"Yes, Henry?"

"Listen to me, Essie." He blew out a frustrated sigh and ran his hands through his thick dark hair. "Female Weres are disappearing...possibly dying. I don't want you anywhere near this."

Part of me melted, but a bigger part took offense. "Look, Hank, I'm not the same naïve girl I was a year ago. I'm trained and I'm very good at what I do. It will give me great pleasure to destroy whoever is doing this and you need me. I'm here whether you want me here or not. So if you don't want me going in blind, hand over what you've got."

He gave me a calculated stare and I met it head on. "You've changed. You're hard."

"Girl's gotta do what a girl's gotta do," I said. He was so wrong about me I wanted to cry, but it was better he thought poorly of me. It would make everything much easier when I left again.

"We've kept it out of the papers," he said in a clipped business-like tone. "Only the Pack knows what's going on. As far as anyone knowing what you're really doing here, it's just me and Junior. I figured you'd be safer that way."

30

"I agree. Do you really think the girls are dead?"

"Don't know," he admitted. "None of those gals are the kind to pick up and disappear. It all seems connected to the modeling agency."

"Yep. The town thinks I'm flighty anyway, so no one will be surprised that I've come home to be a model."

"No one thinks you're flighty except me. The whole town thinks you're the best thing since sliced bread. The modeling thing wasn't the best cover for you, so I told the Pack you've come back so we could work on our issues," he replied casually.

"You did what?" I yelled. "You had no right to tell anyone that kind of crap-assed lie."

"It's a solid cover and it's already done. You can't tell me you haven't had to do a little acting during your undercover stints. This should be a breeze for someone as *skilled* as you," he said smoothly.

I closed my eyes for a moment and sucked in some air. I was a big girl. The fact that people were missing was far larger than the small fact that I would have to pretend to be Hank the Skank's girlfriend again. I could do this. It was a job. He was a job. He meant nothing to me...and I was *not* going to bang him.

"No problem." I smiled and lied. "It will be fun."

His eyes narrowed again and he watched me closely. "Fun?"

"Yep, but won't it be embarrassing for you when I leave again?" I asked sweetly.

"We'll cross that bridge if we come to it," he answered just as sweetly.

Wait. Did he say *if*? Crap, I didn't want to ask him to clarify because if I was wrong, I would look like an idiot and if I was right...OMG. Enough. I had a mission and he would not make me lose focus.

"Files?" I held my hand out and waited.

He gave me a sexy half smirk and my stomach flip-flopped. "You'll get the files after I see you shoot."

"Would you like me to shoot you in your office?" I inquired politely.

"That won't be necessary. Junior would be in charge if you killed me and I don't think he's up to it at the moment." He chuckled and sat on the edge of his *desk of sin*. "Meet me at six at the range. It'll be closed. I don't want anyone to know you're packing."

"No one will know I'm packing, Hank. I carry my gun between my thighs." With that little nugget I got up and left his office before he could respond. The look on his face was priceless, but I was playing with fire. He knew it and I knew it.

***

"What in the Sam Hill was that?" Junior shouted. "She hit every kill zone twice, then blew his balls to Kingdom Come."

"Guns down," Hank said tersely. He walked to the target and examined it. He dropped his head back onto his shoulders and did some deep breathing. He wanted to blow a gasket, but he couldn't. I'd proved him wrong. "Do it again."

"Fine," I said. "Move."

"That's right, boy," Junior yelled. "If you want to keep your nuts, you better haul ass out of there."

I slipped my ear protectors back on and did a repeat performance. Almost. I hit all the kill zones twice and then I completely obliterated the target's testicles.

"I'm having a visceral reaction to that shit," Junior grunted and bent at the waist. "Ease up on the man junk, Essie."

If I wasn't mistaken, *and I wasn't*, Hank was leaning forward too.

"I'm satisfied," Junior said as he packed up his weapons. "She could shoot the teats off a cow in the next county. You two wanna come to the diner and get a bite?"

"No," we said loudly and quickly at the same time.

"Have it your way," Junior said as he moseyed over to the exit. "I'm lockin' the door behind me just in case you two wanna…"

"We don't want to do anything," I said, hoping that came out stronger than it sounded to my own ears. "I have to get home to my granny and my…um, friend Dwayne."

Junior froze and shot his brother a concerned look. Hank barely responded to my possible involvement with another man. Wait. Had me telling him no really worked? I found that hard to believe, and alarmingly I found it depressing. Junior shrugged his massive shoulders and left.

"We have a few more things to go through and then you can get back to your *friend*," Hank said politely.

"Um...okay. I proved I could shoot, which by the way was ridiculous. What else do I have to do to convince you?" I put my gun back into my bag, slapped my hands on my hips and gave him a look.

"Hand to hand." He smirked as he put his gun away.

He was smoking crack if he thought we were going to wrestle. It was all I could do to keep my inner wolf from jumping his bones and flushing my self-respect down the toilet. If I had to actually touch him, I was toast.

"Nope. You already know I can fight. You taught me how to fight. I will not go hand-to- hand with you. Period. Plus, I didn't bring the right clothes," I said, indicating my jeans and boots with great relief.

Without looking at me he tossed me some scraps of material.

"Put them on," he said as he removed his shirt and pulled on a t-shirt. My eyes almost popped out of my head. No one had a right to look like him. The light sprinkling of dark hair on his perfectly tanned chest veed down to the waistband of his jeans in the sexiest way imaginable and made my knees knock. Quickly looking away, I cursed him out viciously inside my head.

The ball of material in my hands looked vaguely familiar. *Hell to the no.* They looked familiar because they were mine. It was the outfit I worked out in the afternoon I left him. I must have thrown it in the laundry and forgotten about it. There was no way in hell I was going to put on booty shorts and a sports bra.

"I can't wear these," I mumbled.

"Suit yourself. We'll go hand to hand in what you have on."

"Is this your last test?" I demanded.

"For the moment." He grinned and shrugged.

He sucked so bad I wanted to smack him. He would have an advantage if I were in boots and jeans. The simple fact that I was far more competitive than rational had not served me well in life and I was about to prove that point again.

"Fine. Turn around."

"Has living in the big city made you self-conscious?" he asked, standing his ground and watching me intently.

"No," I insisted quickly. Nudity meant nothing to Werewolves. A body was a body. We stripped to shift in large groups—it was natural. I wasn't at all self-conscious about my body...it was him. No, it was me. I didn't trust myself and that infuriated me. He meant nothing. So what if I was still attracted to him? He was pretty and built like a Greek god, but he was a cheating loser and I was better off without him. He wanted me to strip? Then I was gonna strip. Slowly.

Turning sideways so I could avoid his eyes, I eased my jeans off my hips and then down my long legs, slipping my cowboy boots off as I went. The air in the gun range was cool and tiny chill bumps covered my body. What was my problem? Well, my inner wolf was one of them. She wanted me to bang him and was making no bones about it. I shoved her down and she pouted. I quickly shed the rest of my clothes. A striptease was going to backfire in a big bad way. I knew his eyes were on me and I yanked on the obscene booty shorts and bra. My fury at myself and him built to a point that I was ready to kick some ass—his, to be more specific.

"I'm ready. Let's go."

I was delighted he found the need to adjust himself in his sweats. His erection would be a disadvantage and even though I didn't care, it meant I still affected him. Considering he was the deadliest fighter I'd ever seen and had at least a hundred pounds on me, I'd take any advantage I could get.

"This isn't going to work," he muttered and stared at the ceiling.

"You chicken?" I taunted.

He was on me so fast I didn't see him coming. Pinned underneath him on the floor, my inner wolf hooker was ecstatic. His hard body pressed against my softer one brought back memories that needed to stay buried. His scent mingled with mine and I closed my eyes and tried to think about the time my third grade teacher threw up in the lunchroom. Oh my hell, that didn't even work. The need to taste him was overwhelming. I was not going to bang him. I was not going to bang him. I was not...

"Why did you leave?" he questioned as he pushed his knee between my legs. "Why?"

His lips were a breath away from mine. It would be so easy to trace them with my tongue. Maybe if I banged him just once it wouldn't count. I didn't have to tell Dwayne. No one needed to know. I'd just bang him and ignore him and then I would...

"Was there someone else?" he demanded.

"Are you high?" I hissed and tried to roll out from under him, but he had me right where he wanted me. Actually, if I was being honest with myself, *which I wasn't,* I was exactly where I wanted to be. "You have some nerve asking me that, you assbuckle."

"Assbuckle?" He chuckled and pressed his body closer to mine, making it difficult to form thought. "You treat me with no respect whatsoever. I'm your alpha."

"I'm no longer part of the Pack," I said. "You're just some random guy now."

His eyes were lit with amusement as he lowered his lips to mine. I jerked my head to the right, inadvertently giving him access to my neck. Of course he knew from experience that it was the most sensitive part of my body. Crapballs. His lips brushed the sensitive skin lightly and my body shuddered with delight in response.

"I could mark you, Essie. Bite you and make you mine forever," he said softly.

"You wouldn't dare," I said in a breathy voice that sounded a little phone sex operator-ish.

"No," he agreed. "When I mark you, it will be because you beg, but I will leave a little gift."

His mouth was on my neck and he sucked. The sensation shot through me like a bullet and went straight to my girlie parts. Thoughts were cloudy, but there was a small part of my brain that knew this was a bad idea...why? Why was this bad? How could something that felt so amazing be wrong? OMG. I knew why this was bad.

With every ounce of strength I had, I raised my knee and introduced it to his man jewels. His grunt of pain was music to my ears as he rolled off of me and curled into a ball.

"I am not yours to play with anymore," I huffed and got to my feet. He was still on the floor. I backed away in case he was bluffing. I knew I'd nailed him, but...

"You are going to explain very soon why your body says one thing and your knee says another," he snapped and got on all fours. "I don't buy that you don't want me and god knows I want you." He continued to breathe unevenly as he worked through the pain I'd inflicted.

I was fine with that. He'd caused me more pain than I'd ever known I could handle. I was glad to give some back.

"You are unbelievable. You either have amnesia or you're the smarmiest buttwank I've ever known. I owe you nothing. I'll be at your office tomorrow morning before I register at the modeling agency and then we can talk on a need only basis. Period."

He was still on the floor and I actually felt a tiny bit bad. However, I was glad he was down and I left before he could come after me and get his payback. This job was sucking so bad and I had a feeling it was only going to get worse.

Chapter 5

"If I told you once I told you twenty times, Blood Sucker. If you hold your needles like that it's gonna be lopsided," Granny chastised Dwayne as they knitted up a storm.

"You're just pissy because I've already knitted twelve scarves to your nine, Fido," Dwayne huffed, knitting like the Devil himself was on his heels.

The living room was a disaster. Yarn, needles and patterns littered the overturned furniture. My BFF and Granny sat on the floor in the middle of the calamity sweating up a storm. Well, Granny sweated. Vampyres didn't have pores. The scarves were hideous—all holey and messy and weird, but there was a ton of them. Completely unable to piece together any probable story of what had happened, I stood in silence and gaped.

"Close your mouth. You'll catch flies," Granny informed me, not even glancing up from the fuchsia thing she was creating.

"Did you bang him?" Dwayne asked while still completely absorbed in his puke green masterpiece. "I have money riding on it."

"No, I didn't bang him," I yelled. "What in the hell happened here?" I hoped my volume and quick change of subject would throw them.

No such luck.

"I say the hickey on your neck proves my bang theory," Dwayne said, held up the horrific scarf and dropped his needles in exhaustion. "I win, Furball."

"Bull honkey," Granny snapped. "My quality is far superior."

"There was nothing in the rules that implied quality," Dwayne stated calmly, secure in his victory.

"What happened to the living room?" I asked as I began to right the furniture.

"Well, we had a little debate," Granny said, eyeing the pile of crap they'd created.

"It turns out Granny has sharper fangs and a slightly better right hook and I'm faster and have a far superior sense of smell," Dwayne informed me.

"That ain't nothing to brag about, Vein Eater," she sniffed indignantly. "Fangs trump smell any day of the week."

"She has a point," I added.

Dwayne laughed and wrapped a pink scarf around his neck. "I can smell species."

This shocked and silenced both me and Granny. I was totally unaware that Vamps could identify species by scent. That was huge. I could scent a shifter and I knew if it was a wolf, but it took more than just smell to correctly identify what kind of shifter.

"I call bullshit," Granny said and wound a baby blue scarf around her neck.

"That was a rabbit that delivered the pizza," Dwayne said and handed me a shiny silver scarf. "You'll need this to cover the welt on your neck."

Ignoring the comment and the ugly, holey neckwear, I zeroed in on Grandma. "You ordered pizza? From Juju?"

Juju was a rabbit shifter and made the best pizza known to man. It was so damn good that every wolf in the surrounding area had voluntarily given up eating rabbit in their animal form. No one would take the risk of accidentally eating Juju. No one.

"Yes, I did and apparently Bat Boy isn't joking. You knew he was a rabbit?" she demanded.

"Of course," Dwayne answered smugly. "And he's boffing a weasel."

"Juju and Sara Mary Munchouse are doing the nasty?" I gasped and dropped down on an upended plaid ottoman. That was too much to stomach. Juju was five feet tall and weighed a hundred pounds sopping wet and Sara Mary was six feet tall and came in at a conservative three hundred. The physical mechanics were mind-boggling. Shoving the images into the far recesses of my brain in the "never pull those up again" section, I got back to the more important issue.

"There's Juju pizza in this house and you didn't tell me?"

"I was a little busy kicking your dead friend's ass," Granny said. "Go help yourself."

"I will," I muttered and hauled tail to the kitchen. It had been a full year since I'd eaten Juju's pizza and my mouth watered at the prospect.

"Junior came by and left you a stack of files," Granny said as she snagged a slice. "He gave your buddy the evil eye till Dwayne asked him if he'd had butt implants and wanted to touch them to make sure they were real."

I choked on my pizza and asked myself yet again why I'd let Dwayne come with me.

"I really wish I'd known he was Hank's older brother. I would have mentioned impaling you on a regular basis," Dwayne said earnestly.

Again, I choked.

"Looks like Hank the Hickey Maker struck again," Granny stated gleefully with a mouthful of double pepperoni.

"What are you talking about?" I demanded. Juju's pizza suddenly tasted like cardboard in my mouth as the reality hit. I had thought they were joking. "Did that hairy dork leave a mark?"

"A big one," Dwayne gushed. "You so banged him."

"I did not bang him. I racked him."

"Whoa," he said, bending at the waist in sympathy. "You're really mean."

"You know what?" I shouted. "I'm not mean. He's mean. Mean and stupid and full of himself and wanky and fat and ugly and mean and dumb and…"

"And you want to bang him?" Dwayne added unhelpfully.

I dropped to the floor in defeat. Pizza wasn't going to help. The only thing that would help at this point was running again, but that was out of the question. I had a job. Maybe I got it under false pretenses, but I was a good agent and I knew it. I would find out what was happening here, end it and then I was gone. I had to leave or I would fall back into a trap that would tear my heart to shreds from the inside out. "Yes. Yes, I want to bang him, but I won't. I have a small amount of self-respect left and I plan to hang onto it for dear life."

"Honey child, what happened?" Granny asked as she slid down the wall and plopped down on the floor next to me. "What could have been so awful?"

Dwayne got comfortable on the other side of me. Usually being sandwiched by people made me itch, but these people loved me...warts and all.

"I don't want to talk about it," I mumbled.

"Sometimes talking about painful things helps, Essie," Dwayne said gently. "I'll go first. About two hundred and fifty years ago during a great famine there wasn't enough food for the humans and they got really skinny and tasted like burnt peas and rancid hummus—it was harder than hell for a Vampyre to eat. I accidentally killed a lovely fellow from my glee club and I just felt awful about it, so I started drinking pig's blood and let me tell you—that was gross. Pigs are cute—well, piglets are and all I could find were damn piglets. They would stare at me with those little piglet eyes...I love *Charlotte's Web*. The book is waaay better than the movie. Don't you think? Anyhoo, I got so upset, I moved on to sheep. Several Vamps I knew were even...wait, what were we talking about?" Dwayne asked.

"I honestly don't remember," I whispered fearfully as I prayed he wouldn't continue his bizarre confession.

Granny was quiet. She was either contemplating Dwayne's story or trying to come up with one that would top his. I shivered as I realized she would go to her standard fare and regale us with anecdotes from her stripping days, which could easily morph into a demonstration...I had to stop the madness before it began.

"I have to read files tonight," I explained as I un-wedged myself. "You should take Dwayne out and show him the town—maybe go to the beach or stroll down Main Street."

"She's got that covered," Dwayne squealed. "We're going to a drag show!"

"In Hung?" I asked Granny. "There's a drag club in Hung?"

"Three," she replied. "And two Shifter strip clubs."

How did I not know this? I bit down hard on the inside of my cheek. If she was still disrobing in public, I didn't want to know. There wasn't a therapist alive that could wipe that image out of my brain.

"Okay, um...you guys have fun, and Dwayne, if you're going to eat you need to be discreet. We're used to a variety of Shifters down here, but not Vamps."

"Don't you worry about nothin'. I've got his back," Granny said. "Anyone calls him a blood sucker or homo will answer to my fist, my boot and my Taser." With that lovely nugget she left the room to get gussied up.

"Oh my god, if I were into women, I'd marry your granny so fast." Dwayne preened in front of the mirror.

"Um...awesome," I gagged. "If you say anything that foul again, you're walking back to Chicago. Tonight."

"It would be a little weird to be your grandpa," he mused.

"Do you do it on purpose?"

"Do what?" he asked, confused.

"Leave me with images that no amount of psychotherapy could remove? Burnt peas and rancid hummus are now seared into my brain along with you and Granny and the fact that you clearly sang in a glee club."

"Those were difficult times, Essie. You think you have problems? Try running naked through coals while being pelted with boar's teeth."

Nothing. I had nothing.

"You ready, Dead Boy?" Granny asked.

Oh, hell to the no...She was dressed in a boob tube, peasant skirt and sequined kitten heels. Weres did not look their age. Granny could easily pass for mid-forties even

41

though she was in her eighties, but a boob tube was wrong on anyone over five.

"Granny, I really don't think you should…"

"You are smokin' hawt," Dwayne yelled as he fist bumped my elderly grandma.

What the hell was I thinking? He had more than two hundred years on both of us. Weird was my new normal—accept and continue.

"Okay then, try not to get arrested and be home before sunup," I muttered and grabbed the stack of files.

"You sure you don't wanna come? Bennett Pombell does a mean Cher," she explained as she twisted her hair up and shoved three chopsticks into it.

Bennett Pombell was an upstanding panther Shifter with seven kids and a shrew of a wife…accept and continue. "I'm good. Got work to do."

"Does anyone do Gaga?" Dwayne asked as they walked out the front door.

"No, maybe you should," she suggested.

"Do you think I'd be good?" he gushed.

"You'd be wonderful. I have some wigs from my stripping days in the garage. You wanna see?" Granny asked a deliriously excited Dwayne.

"Lead on, my Queen. Lead on."

***

The files were meticulous. I had assumed Hank was good. He was an alpha of a large and very happy Pack, but I had no clue what an amazing detective he was…not that I'd tell him. Ever.

I'd spent the better part of four hours poring over the files before Granny and Lady Gaga, *aka Dwayne in full on drag,* got home. Apparently Dwayne was the new star of the Hung drag circuit and Granny was now his manager. They were booked solid for the week.

After seeing a replay of Dwayne's performance on Granny's phone and then watching him perform the highlights in the kitchen, we went to bed. Dwayne was a truly amazing Gaga. They both made me swear on a stack of Bibles I would catch a performance this week. I promised I'd try.

Chapter 6

"You know, if you would dress up like Beyonce we could do a killer version of *Telephone*," Dwayne said as he handed me a glass of fresh squeezed OJ and a blueberry muffin he had baked for breakfast.

"Why do you bake if you don't eat?" I asked.

"It relaxes me. Are you ignoring my suggestion?"

"Yes. Yes, I am."

I bit into the muffin and my eyes rolled back in ecstasy. My Vampyre could bake.

"I'd like you to consider my brilliant idea."

"Dwayne, the point of drag is that men dress up as women. I am a woman with real boobs."

"True, and your boobs are fabu. You're hotter than hell and I'd love to see you in some gold lamé booty shorts and a sequined bra. I think it would be therapeutic for you."

"I have about fourteen sequined bras," Granny chimed in as she sauntered into the kitchen and grabbed a muffin. "Some of them are nipple-less, but I'm sure I have a few that would work."

"On that note, I'm outta here," I said. I grabbed the files and an extra muffin. "Can you two stay out of trouble?" The innocent looks on their faces set my allergic-to-bullshit radar off, but I didn't have time to babysit them. "Just don't get arrested," I muttered and hurried out the door before Granny insisted I try on her sparkly brassieres.

"Lunch?" Dwayne yelled as I ran to my car.

"Yep. I'll call you."

***

The office was a disaster—like someone had ransacked it, but I realized as Junior paced the room it was him. He was knocking everything off the tables and walls. He was alarmingly animated and unconsciously destructive. For my own safety, I pressed myself against the door and waited.

"Listen to me, Essie," Junior pleaded. "You have got to bang my brother. Just bang the living hell out of him."

"I'm sorry. What did you just say?" The sheriff's office, which wasn't large to start with, had just gotten smaller. It felt as if the walls were closing in and I was going to get squished like a bug. Was he for real? Was there anyone in Hung who didn't want me to bang Hank? Well, I knew of three people who certainly didn't want me to bang him...

"It's been a year since he got laaaahhhhhhh, I mean, um...Hang Man is my baby brother's favorite—you know, ahhh game and I'm going to suggest making it a professional Olympic sport and, ah..." Junior paled considerably and inched his huge body toward the exit, making it very obvious that the potential bangee had entered the room.

"Junior, I can handle my own affairs," Hank ground out. "If you'd like to live to see tomorrow, I'd suggest you take the rest of the day off."

"Outstanding suggestion, bro," Junior agreed shakily as he slunk out of the office. "Should I straighten up in here?"

"No. I'll take care of it." Hank groaned as he took in the mess Junior had made.

I closed my eyes for a brief moment before I really looked at Hank. If Junior was telling the truth, Hank hadn't gotten laid in a year. That made no sense whatsoever and Junior was famous for stretching the truth, so I decided to wrestle with that another time—as in never. However, my lady bits and my inner wolf danced with joy. *Stop.* Not here to bang the sheriff. Here to work. Period. I was a big girl and I could work with him. I was beyond impressed with his attention to detail in the reports and he had some theories I hadn't considered. He was a colleague and I was a professional. Nothing more. Nothing less. Plastering a pleasant smile on my face I opened my eyes and... Mother humpin' cowballs... I quickly grabbed the back of a chair so I would continue to appear as if I could stand on my own feet.

He wore a shirt I had given him. A lightweight green Henley that matched his eyes perfectly. Not only was he color-coordinated, he was mouthwatering. His muscles strained against the fabric and begged to be licked. *Wait. What?* I mentally smacked the tar out of my inner wolf and prayed to all the angels and saints for strength. There would be no licking today.

"The files were very thorough," I choked out as I breezed past him into his office. Blindly sitting on the first thing my butt could find, I realized I was perched on a pile of old newspapers. Nice.

"You comfortable?" he asked with a smirk.

"Extremely, thank you." I'd be damned if I was going to let on that I hadn't meant to slap my rear end down on a large stack of paper. "Newspapers are good for posture and lower back," I mumbled and then bit down on my tongue before I spewed out more inane crap. Why did I let him affect me this way? I was over him. Done. Over and done.

Liar, liar, pants on fire.

"So, thoughts?" He settled in behind his desk and waited.

"About?" I asked politely, hoping desperately I'd not uttered any of my incriminating inner monologue aloud.

"The case?" He grinned and raised an eyebrow.

His words were like an ice cold shower. Thank God. The case. I could handle talking business. I was good at that. It was everything else I had problems with.

"The files are good, but why is there very little about the humans running the agency?"

He paused and gave me a smile that resembled a grimace. "They're not local. Three human males came in from New York and we're having a hell of a time tracing them."

"Have you put them in the WTF database?"

"Yep. They're drawing blanks too."

"Interesting and not good," I said as I pulled out the thinnest file and scanned it. "The bodies haven't been found and the scent trails disappeared. I find that very difficult to believe. How much of a time lapse was there before the searches started?"

"The first victim was three days," he said tightly and ran his hand through his hair in frustration. "After that it was immediate once we learned they were missing."

"And you found nothing?"

"Isn't that obvious, Miss Hotshot?" he snapped. "This is driving me crazier than you sitting across the desk from me. These are my people and I'm supposed to protect them. I can't even find them," he bellowed. His concern for our missing Pack members and his fury at being unable to locate them filled the room.

I was simply being professional, but felt like a jerk. Again, I was reminded that I was on a case with huge conflicts of interest. Maintaining distance and objectivity were going to be difficult—knowing the missing women was hard enough. Working with the person who my inner wolf was convinced was her true mate was pure hell.

Wolves could mate with whomever they wanted. Some lasted and some didn't. We had long lives and overactive sex drives. If you didn't find your true mate, *a fairy tale I tended to not believe*, you often had several relationships during a lifetime.

True mates belonged together...supposedly. If they had crossed paths, even as children, they would never be happy with someone else. Which proved my theory that Hank wasn't my true mate. If he had been, he couldn't have cheated on me. It was a virtual, medical and erectile impossibility for a male Were to cheat on his true mate. Junior was full of crap. There was no way in hell Hank the Tank wasn't getting some. He was the most over-sexed Were I knew...not that I knew about any other Weres sex lives. I'd only ever been with the smug buttknuckle who was staring at me. I was pathetic. I just needed to get back out there. It was beside the point that I hadn't dated or even shown a modicum of interest in anyone since I'd left him...but I'd been busy. Extremely busy. Becoming a killing machine for WTF had been a ton of work and then I...

"Look," Hank said, thankfully cutting my ridiculous thought process short. "I don't want you here because it's not safe. As much as I want to take you over my knee and spank the hell out of you for leaving, I don't think I could go on if something happened to you. So you will report your every move to me or I will be on you so fast it will hurt. Do you understand?"

"Do you understand that I've done things far more dangerous than this?" I shot back, ignoring the fact that the spanking thing was kind of a turn-on.

"Considering we don't know what we're dealing with that's a bold and risky statement to make." He crossed over to me and obliterated my personal space. Short of straddling the newspapers in a miniskirt to back off of them I was stuck. I hated being wrong, but I was smart enough to admit when I was. Cocky got you killed. I had no plans to die anytime in the near future.

"Fine," I said and tried to push him away to little avail. "That was stupid and arrogant. I will go into this carefully and I will take as few risks as possible. As far as constant communication...I'll do my best, but you have to let me do my job."

"What exactly do you plan on doing?" he demanded. The thick muscles in his neck were taut and I knew it was taking everything he had not to run my Wolfy ass out of town.

"I plan to fly by the seat of my pants," I explained logically as his jaw clenched along with his fists. "Since we don't know who or what we're dealing with yet, I can't give you solids. However, I do promise if it looks dangerous I won't go in without backup."

"I call bullshit."

"What?"

"You've gone into situations four times in the last year without backup. The last time you were almost killed."

"Do I look dead to you?" I hissed. He had some nerve. I'd done all that because lives were at stake. Twice it had been children's lives.

"You were lucky—and luck runs out."

"I beg to differ, butthole." *Damn it, butthole made me sound like an incompetent child. I should have said asshole...* "Luck had nothing to do with it. I'm skilled and I made all of those sons of bitches hurt bad. And how in the hell do you know all this?" I barked.

"Essie, I am always aware of what belongs to me."

"Well, as lovely as that is," I sneered, "I don't belong to you. I belong to me and me alone. You need to move before I introduce your nuts to my fist. I'd use my knee on your man bits, but I'm wearing a miniskirt and I refuse to flash my goodies at you. I did my research and wore something model-y because that's how I roll. Plus, I'm more apt to get the gig if I flash some leg and tit. So move. Now."

Hank yanked me to my feet and flush against his hard body. "You will wear a wire."

Gritting my teeth and forbidding myself to rub all over him like a cat in heat, I nodded curtly.

"I will wear a wire."

"Lift your shirt and unbutton that scrap of material you call a skirt," he instructed.

"Not on your life."

He gave me a lazy grin and shrugged. "Fine. Can you wire yourself?"

"Of course," I snapped. How hard could it be to hide a damn wire? I snatched the pack from his hand and went to work. He stepped back and watched with interest.

I shoved the pack down the back of my panties and clipped it. I then wound the wire around my body with shaking hands. I eased the cord and mic under my bra and attached it to my bra cup.

"Done," I said triumphantly.

"Look in the mirror."

I glanced over at my reflection and realized someone would have to be blind not to know I was wearing a wire. Crapcrapcrap. It was a mess.

Sucking in a huge breath and remembering why I was actually here, I gave in. "Help me."

"Please?" He gave me the sexiest evil grin and cocked his head to the right.

"Please," I ground out between clenched teeth.

"My pleasure. Lift your shirt and unbutton your skirt."

I did.

His warm calloused hands on my bare skin as he readjusted the wire and taped it to my body were a mixture of heaven and hell. His clean sexy scent invaded my nose and I held my breath. It was all I could do to not turn around, slam him to the ground and have my way with him.

"I need to move the pack lower," he said gruffly and slid his hands into the back of my panties.

We both froze and I gasped. Air hissed from between his lips and it burned my neck. A small fire had ignited low in my belly and began to travel quickly through me. His hand slid down and cupped my bare ass and his head dropped to my shoulder. His lips grazed my neck and I shuddered. I was quite sure this wasn't a normal cop procedure, but I couldn't bring myself to make him stop. It was the first time I'd felt alive in a year and I hated that he made me feel this way. My gums ached and I knew my fangs were very close to the surface. His had arrived and I felt them scrape my skin.

"You have to stop," I begged, but did nothing to make him. If I wasn't mistaken, *and I wasn't*, I was fairly sure I'd readjusted so my butt was more firmly in his hand. What was wrong with me?

"Do you really want me to?" he whispered in my ear, sending chills down my spine and my girlie parts into a tailspin. God, if he kept talking I would come apart by his voice alone. He had that sexy Werewolf magic thing down pat.

I nodded my head yes, afraid that my mouth would tell him to bend me over his desk and make me see Jesus.

"You have no idea how hard it is, pun intended, for me to let you go right now...but I will. We have to find out what is happening to our people and end it, but this conversation is far from over. Do you understand me?"

I nodded again, terrified that I was going to beg for a quickie before I went out and kicked some ass.

He slowly slid his hand from my panties and my body felt bereft. I may have nodded yes, but the rest of this conversation was never going to happen. He already had my broken heart. I'd given it to him years ago. There was no way in hell he was going to take my pride.

"Your appointment is in fifteen minutes. You'll meet me for lunch afterward. Everyone in town believes we're back together."

One last time I nodded, afraid if I spoke I might cry. I stared at him for a long moment. His strength and power were evident in every move he made. At one point in time I basked in it, but now I just admired it from afar. He was a force of nature—a true alpha. I worried for a brief moment that if he couldn't find our people that I might not be able to either, but I pushed that thought aside. I might be a screw-up in life, but I was damn good at finding trouble…it came to me. And now because I was prepared I could destroy it—and I would.

I walked slowly toward Hank. His quick intake of breath brought a small smile to my lips. He was right. Who knew what I was getting into? Today might be my last and I wanted to do one small thing, just in case. He stood as still as a statue as I pressed my lips to his. I breathed in his masculine scent and I was home. It was just too damn bad his lips liked other necks and chests and asses. But for one brief moment I pretended he was still mine.

I pulled back and moved to leave.

"The conversation is not over, Essie," he warned.

I turned and walked away. There was little else I could do.

Chapter 7

The agency was on Main Street next to the cozy used bookstore that I had practically lived in as a kid. The sense of home I felt in this little sleepy town made my heart thump painfully. However, this was no longer my home. I had left by choice and I would leave again. Glancing around, I zeroed in on the modeling agency. Damn, it was ugly. Models Mania was sleek and modern and didn't fit into my charming town at all. The name was beyond stupid too. I let go of my attitude, hunkered down in my smelly car and reviewed what I knew.

It was run by three human males from New York: Peter Pyre, Paul Tinder and Puck Flare. The names were bizarre and slightly unfortunate. I had concluded that they were aliases since we couldn't trace them. They clearly thought they were hot, considering they all had forms of fire as their surnames. I bit back a groan and read on.

There was no indication that the Three Ps knew that shifters existed, but I didn't buy it. No human women had gone missing and I didn't believe it was a coincidence. It was risky to imply that the Council, since they had backed the agency, had let the humans in on our secret, but the evidence was pointing that way.

It appeared that the missing girls had been recruited. Did the humans recruit them or did the Council? I flipped through the file and found nothing. I quickly texted Granny and told her to call around and find out the buzz on the recruiting. She texted back that she would get on it after she and Dwayne finished a round of paintball. She promised to have some info at lunch. I hoped to hell they'd at least gone out to the deserted beach to shoot each other with paint, but my expectation was that they were attacking each other in broad daylight in the quaint confines of her neighborhood. So much for no arrests…

The agency looked empty, but I had an appointment in five minutes. I grabbed a cup and filled it with water from a bottle I found under the seat. I hoped to come out of there with some fingerprints on it.

Checking my makeup in the rearview mirror, I was satisfied. The fact that I could pass for a model didn't thrill me. My looks were inherited. Actually, most Shifters were pretty people. While being attractive had gotten in the way occasionally during training, it certainly came in handy today. I pushed up my boobs, hiked up my skirt, checked my wire and went into battle.

"Hello," I called out in the darkened office. It was obsessively neat and smelled odd. I couldn't place it. I wandered to the counter and examined the stack of beauty products. I found the culprit—self tanner. It had the strangest odor. I slipped one in my purse and took a seat on the white leather settee.

"Be right with you," a rough male voice called from the back.

The sound of a woman giggling in the back room made my stomach lurch. I recognized the laugh and I had to breathe deeply to keep my claws from coming out. Literally. I despised the owner of the laugh. Damn it, if one of them was back there, I'd bet money all three were. Of course they were here. They were beautiful on the outside, even if they were nasty evil home wreckers. *Whoa, Nelly.* Hank had a choice. It took two to tango, or in their case, four. I might hate them, but if it hadn't been them, he would have most certainly fooled around with someone else. Maybe I should thank them…nope, that was never going to happen. I could have mated with him and found out what a cheating dog he was after the fact. As much as I wanted to shift into my wolf and tear those girls apart, they had actually done me a favor.

"What's she doing here?" a nasal voice demanded. "I didn't give her an appointment."

I was right, it was Tina #1 and she was not pleased to see me. She was one of three. They were all named Tina and they had all had a hand in ruining my life. She'd clearly moved on from Hank because she was draped over a large attractive man like a barnacle.

Large Man shoved Tina #1 off of him and stepped forward with his hand extended and a slick smile on his pretty face. "Please excuse the help — it's difficult to find subordinates with manners these days. I'm Puck Flare, owner and talent coordinator of the agency. It's lovely to meet you. You must be Essie McGee."

Tina #1 positively seethed. As delighted as I was with the way he shot her down, it was also appalling. Not to mention it stymied me why she would let a mere human treat her so poorly. She was a Werewolf and we rarely mixed with humans in a romantic or sexual way.

"I am." An unexplainable feeling of uneasiness shot through me as I extended my hand. I plastered on a smile that I prayed didn't look fake and took his hand in mine. He felt a bit cool for a human, but he was definitely human.

"I do believe we could book you on some very big jobs." He circled me like I was a car he was considering.

"Great. That's great," I masked my unease and jumped up and down a bit to appear as vapid as possible. Tina #1 hissed and narrowed her eyes.

"Tina, don't you have work to do?" Puck snapped.

She nodded meekly and went to the back room.

"Sorry about that, my dear," he said. "She wants to model, but she's a bit too short. Let's have you fill out some paperwork and then we'll take some Polaroids for your file. Do you have a head shot or a portfolio?"

"Um, no...I've just always thought this might be fun and I'm into travel and being in magazines," I gushed.

"That's wonderful. You're available to travel? No jealous boyfriends or silly little day jobs to speak of?"

"Nope. Free and clear. No job and definitely no boyfriend," I said, and wondered what Hank thought about my answer. I knew he was listening through an earpiece at the station. "Can I ask a few questions, Mr. Flare?"

"Of course, and please call me Puck."

"Sure, um…Puck. What kind of jobs could I book with you? And what's the pay?"

"Dear girl, for someone with your looks and body, the sky is the limit."

He made me feel dirty and I was positive he was involved with the missing girls, but I had no clue how or why. I giggled and searched my repertoire for something girlie and flirty…I unconsciously did the Dwayne hair flick over my shoulder and almost burst out laughing. Concentrating hard, I held back my eye roll and the strong need to call Puck something that rhymed with his name and ended in "er".

"Wow," I cooed and did a little shimmy. "That's the total bomb! When do I start?"

He chuckled and bought my vapid enthusiasm hook, line, and sinker. "We'll start tomorrow. However, you're a bit pale," he said as he walked to the mountain of beauty products on the counter. "How about you do a little self tanner tonight so your shots tomorrow will be as sexy as you are."

"Oh Puck," I gasped and tossed my hair like an imbecile. "You're such a charmer."

"I do my best." He covertly began to flex his muscles and it was all I could do not to throw up in my mouth. "You need to cover your entire body, if you know what I mean." He gave me a smarmy smile and winked.

'Ohhhhhh, that's hot," I cooed.

He handed me the paperwork and I posed for a few Polaroid shots.

"Well, that's about it for now, dear."

Dangit, I needed more info from the pervert…

"What about the others?" I asked as I pulled out my phone.

"What others?" he asked, alarmed.

"The other owners. Don't they have to approve me too?" I asked innocently as he visibly relaxed.

"Oh no," he bragged. "I'm in charge. What I say goes. Anyway, they're off on assignments with some other models."

"Cool," I squealed. "Can I take your picture? You are so hot my friends are going to die."

His ego was huge and he grinned. "Of course, dear."

"Hold this," I blew him a kiss and handed him my cup. "All my friends' bosses are old and fat. I am gonna rub your hotness in in a big way."

"Shall I flex?" he asked as he waggled his eyebrows.

Oh my god he was a loser, but I got his fingerprints on my cup. "Absolutely, but don't be surprised if I faint from your total smokin' manliness," I said in the sexiest voice I could pull out of my butt.

"You are a delightful young woman." He leered and stepped into my personal space. "You are going to be a very desired model."

I took my cup from his hand and stepped back. Breathlessly I stuttered, "What time do I start tomorrow?"

"Be here at ten, dear. And bring an overnight bag just in case. There's a chance you might book a whirlwind gig in New York and we'll have to leave immediately."

"Awesome," I squealed and hustled to the door. "I'll see you tomorrow!"

"Yes, dear. Tomorrow."

As I quickly made my way to the exit, I heard something large and glass shatter in the back room accompanied with a string of swear words from the lovely Tina #1. Puck Flare's eyes narrowed frighteningly as he marched back to investigate. Tina #1 was one of my least favorite people in the world, but I actually felt fear for her. I considered following him back to diffuse the situation, but I could not under any circumstances blow my cover. Innocent women's lives were possibly at stake—or at least their dead bodies.

Besides, I was sure he wouldn't harm Tina #1 with me having witnessed their tiff… I raced to my car and texted Junior. I told him to stop by the agency and buy some products for his mom. I explained the situation and told him to go immediately. He texted back he would.

As much as I wanted to tear Tina #1's limbs from her body, I didn't want to knowingly be responsible for someone harming her. I wanted that honor for myself...

Chapter 8

There was no missing them. Dwayne's bald head and face were dotted with purple and green paint specks, making him look diseased. Granny was wearing a greenish hued blush and her left eyebrow was royal blue. Clearly, protective headgear during paint ball wars wasn't necessary for them.

I rolled my eyes and sat down in the booth. Casey's honky-tonk was a hole in the wall diner a block from the beach. It was a total dive and one of my favorite places in town. The food was awesome and the human owner loved all the locals, so much so that she often threw startled tourists out when there wasn't a table available for one of her regulars.

"You do realize you look ridiculous," I said as I pulled out my phone and snapped a few blackmail shots.

"Essie," Dwayne said as he bounced in his seat. "Granny is going to take me to a football game in the fall."

"The Georgia Vultures?"

"Yep," Granny said. "I got some season tickets real cheap."

"That's not a big surprise." I laughed. "They lost every game last season."

"Who cares? Hot guys in tight white pants with grease paint under their eyes grabbing each other's asses and... Oh my GOD," Dwayne squealed, making me jump and slap my hands over my ears. "What are you doing here, Jeff?"

Who in the hell was Jeff?

"Actually, Dwayne, my name is Hank."

The sexy bane of my existence stood next to the table with a grin on his face that would melt hearts, but not mine. One mystery solved. The pieces fell together with sickening clarity. Dwayne was Hank's informant. Dwayne had been giving up the goods on me for a year to the assmunch who had cheated on me.

"Oh sweet Jesus, Essie, I am so sorry," Dwayne gasped, going as green as the paint dots on his head.

"It's alright, Dwayne," I said as I stared daggers at Hank. "There wasn't much to tell."

"Oh, but there was," Dwayne moaned and placed his hand over his mouth. "He knows...oh god, I can't even say it."

What in the hell had he told Hank? My stomach roiled and my appetite disappeared.

"However," Dwayne said carefully as he recovered from his shock. "The whole thing is kind of hot in a reality TV show kind of way. Don't you think so, Essie?"

"No. I don't," I snapped.

Granny was quiet and watched the exchange with great interest. Where was her loyalty? She was supposed to stand up and cold cock Hank. Instead, she had a sneaky little grin on her face. I pretty much hated everybody right now and I still had no clue what Dwayne had told Hank.

"You are not welcome here," I hissed at him. "Go away. I will talk to you after I have lunch with the people I love." For a brief second I could have sworn pain flashed in his eyes, but it had to be the sun streaming through the windows. He was a heartless wanker, obsessed with what he thought he owned.

"Nope." He grinned and wedged his huge body into the booth next to Granny, who patted him on the head with affection. I was so going to divorce her. "We have things to discuss and time is of the essence."

He was right, which only made me hate him more.

"Fine. Talk and leave."

"Essie, your boob is kind of falling out of your top," Dwayne announced loud enough for all the tables in the restaurant to hear. All eyes shot to my boobs. Hank quickly leaned across the table and covered my chest with his bare hands. A zing shot right through me and my evil traitorous nipples hardened with delight. Hank's grin almost sent me into meltdown. The kind where I killed him, but first I would stick my tongue down his throat and ride him till he was blind.

Shoving him off and grabbing a napkin, I covered my tatas and raced to the bathroom. I had a sundress in my bag. Being an agent had taught me to always carry something extra to wear. No one liked sitting around in blood-spattered or bullet-riddled clothes.

The bathroom of Casey's honky-tonk was an anomaly. The restaurant was tiny but the ladies room was huge — six Pepto Bismol colored stalls and a diaper changing station. I went to the farthest stall and locked myself in. Peeling off the slutty outfit, I realized I was still wired. Not knowing if I would need it again today I left it taped to my body and pulled my sexy but comfy sundress over my head.

I leaned against the cool wall and tried to decipher my feelings. Why was I so angry with Hank if he didn't mean anything to me? Maybe because I was still madly in love with him… No. I was stronger than that. I had more pride. He had cheated on me with the three Tinas and I had seen the results with my own eyes. I deserved someone who wanted only me. Was I nuts?

The magnitude of what I still felt for him was confusing. Maybe I should have talked to him—did he get cold feet and make a mistake? Mistake was mild for what he did. However, the girl I was a year ago only knew how to run. The woman I'd become might not have, but it was fruitless to be consumed with what ifs.

"I can't believe she came back," a voice hissed. "I was sure she'd never set foot in Hung again."

"I saw her today," Tina #1 said. "She was hitting on Puck."

"Clearly we didn't do a good enough job," Tina #2 snapped angrily.

Son of a...why couldn't I catch a break? The Tinas had entered the bathroom and they were talking about me. Should I step out and beat the hell out of them? No. That would be childish and possibly messy. I liked my sundress and, quite honestly, Hank deserved my anger more than they did. After a short internal debate with my inner wolf, *who wanted to kill them*, I decided to stand on the toilet so my feet weren't spotted and listen to what the vipers said...They might have some information on the missing girls. Tina #1 was working at the modeling agency.

"Oh, please," Tina #2 griped. "You're all just pissed because none of us could bag Hank."

Wait. What?

"He's a fool. I literally showed up at his house naked the day after she took off and he kicked me out. No one kicks me out when I'm naked," Tina #1 ground out with fury.

The other Tinas laughed and Tina #1 growled. I was missing a piece of info and my stomach dropped, making me feel ill.

"I vote we give each other hickeys all over our bodies again, show her and tell her he did it. She bought it last time. She's so stupid she'll buy it again."

"Do you remember how she sobbed when we showed her what her boyfriend did to us? It was so much fun. I haven't been able to make anyone cry like that in a year," Tina #3 gushed.

"I actually kind of enjoyed giving you all hickeys," Tina #3 said.

"Are you gay?" Tina #2 demanded.

"No, we were drunk so it didn't count," Tina #3 shot back.

"Look, if she hits on Puck again, I'll give both of you hickeys on your faces to get rid of her. I don't see why men are so attracted to her," Tina #1 spat.

"Because she's beautiful," Tina #3 groused. "Let her have Hank. I never really wanted him anyway."

"Liar," Tina #2 purred. "Everyone red-blooded female Were wants that man. He's the alpha and he's sex on a stick. You're still completely hung up on him."

"Speak for yourself. We have to go back to the agency and get back to work. Those fiery boys are major taskmasters." Tina #1 giggled.

My body felt hot and cold at the same time. I wanted to scream and cry and crawl out of my skin. The need to shift and run until there was no feeling left in me was intense. How had I made a mistake like this? Why had I believed them? The tears rolled unchecked down my cheeks. I could not go back to the table.

I heard them leave and I let the sobs roll through my body. The sounds I made were foreign. I thought my heart had broken a year ago, but I was wrong. It was shattering now and it was no one's fault but mine.

The Tinas were right. I was stupid. I had destroyed the best thing in my life by jumping to conclusions and I was too embarrassed to come clean at this point. Hank deserved someone far better than me. Oh my god, the thought of him finding love and happiness with someone else was horrifying, but I owed him that after how childish and selfish I'd been. I just needed to get through the next week. I would treat him kinder and try and leave as friends. As much as I hated the reality of him with someone else, I loved him enough to want that to happen.

I'd get through lunch and discuss my meeting with Puck Flame and then I'd shift and go for a long run on the beach. I had a whole day to kill before I could work on the case again and I needed to clear my mind and try to forgive myself for being the worst person in the world. I had a feeling that would take decades...

I splashed my face with cold water and tried to fix my hair. My hands shook and tears kept leaking from my eyes. *Pull yourself together. This was your fault. It's done and you lose. Grow up and move on.*

My inner wolf prowled restlessly inside me and I promised her we'd run later. I dabbed my eyes, pinched my cheeks for some color and plastered on a smile that would never reach my eyes again. I could do this.

The lunch crowd had slimmed out and I noticed Dwayne and Granny had left. The hair on the back of my neck stood up. Maybe I should go for a run *now*... Hank

61

was still in the booth and he looked ready to explode. Crapcrapcrap.

I owed him an explanation. I was a big enough girl to do the right thing. I had no clue where Granny and Dwayne went, but something was way off. Had Granny read him the riot act? God, I hoped not. It was me that deserved the riot act. If she had pissed Hank off, why would she have left me to deal with it alone? I glanced wildly around the diner and noticed all the shifters had left. Only humans remained. I waved at a few people I knew and dragged my feet back to the booth.

"Um...hi. Where did Granny and Dwayne go?" I asked.

Hank said nothing. His hands were clenched and his jaw was tight.

"Did you order yet? I didn't order before you got here and I'm kind of hungry, but not really. Actually the thought of swallowing food is nauseating right now, but if you want to eat and discuss the case I can sit here. I could drink some water or a soda or I could go and get my..."

"Sit," Hank instructed tersely.

I did.

"I think that Puck Flame is definitely dirty and I think the Tinas are possibly recruiting for him and his partners. I got his prints on my cup and I'm sure he's using an alias. And, um, I'm going back in the morning, but I'm sure you know that because you were listening at the station."

Hank slowly removed the transmitter from his ear and laid it on the table in front of me. My gut burned and my palms began to sweat. Oh my hell, I was still wearing the wire. He heard everything in the bathroom and he hated me. I wasn't going to get the chance to tell him what a loser I was because he already knew. The need to run was almost overwhelming, but this time I would stay until I was told to go.

Inhaling a deep breath, I gently touched his hand. He didn't take mine, but at least he didn't yank his away. "I am so sorry," I whispered brokenly. "I made a terrible mistake and I'm just so very sorry."

He refused to look at me and I didn't blame him. I didn't want to look at me either. I slid out of the booth and stood. I knew we would have to work together to solve the crime, but I could give him his space when we weren't working. The tiny pieces that were left of my heart tore at my insides.

"I'll check in tomorrow morning before my appointment." I moved to leave, but his hand snaked out and captured my wrist in a vise-like hold.

"If you think you're about to run again, you have another thing coming." His voice was low and furious.

"Let go of my wrist," I said as I tried to hold back tears. "I promise I won't run."

"Your promises aren't really worth much, Essie," he said finally, raising his eyes to mine. "If we weren't in a public place I'd handcuff you to me."

Even though I knew he wanted to lay into me, the thought of being handcuffed to him sent excited chills through me. *I had clearly lost it.* I deserved anything he had to say. It couldn't be any worse than all the things I was saying to myself.

"I have spent a year wondering what I had done to you that was so bad you would leave and I had to hear it like this? You distrusted me so much that you would think I had covered several women's bodies in hickeys?" He was flabbergasted. When I heard him say it out loud, I had to admit I was too. How could I have been so reckless and dumb?

"I..."

"You made us miss out on a year of our lives together because you believed a lie."

"I'm sorry," I said so quietly I almost couldn't hear it.

"Sorry is not cutting it right now. Come with me," he said gruffly.

"Where are we going?" I gasped as he dragged me out of the diner.

He stopped and ran his hands through his hair and exhaled an angry frustrated sigh. "To my house. You've denied both of us for a year and it's time to do something about that."

"You can't possibly want to have sex after what I did," I stammered and backed away.

"Who said anything about sex?" He grinned and my tummy flipped.

"I just thought…"

"You need to stop thinking, Essie. It just gets you into trouble. Get on the bike."

His huge Harley was in the parking lot and I stumbled toward it. He lifted me like I weighed nothing and plopped me down on the seat. He straddled the bike and started it up. It purred and rumbled between my shaking legs.

"Hold on, little girl. It's going to be a bumpy ride—a very bumpy ride."

Chapter 9

His house looked the same as the day I left. A book I had been reading was still on the coffee table and all the feminine touches I had added remained. When I had first moved in it was a total man cave, but Hank was thrilled to let my personality and things join his. The house was a perfect little bungalow tucked away on a private beach on the outskirts of Hung. We had spent many nights wishing on stars and making plans for the future.

I had loved him since high school. He was four years older and watched me from afar until I graduated college. He made his moves quickly and there was no looking back for either of us. I loved him completely—his strength, compassion and smokin' hot butt just killed me. I couldn't believe someone like him wanted someone like me. He was as deadly as he was kind—a rare combination for a Shifter. He was a tough but fair alpha of the Pack and had only been challenged once since he took over for his father. The challenge was horrifying. It was the first time I'd seen Hank fight. My alpha was mesmerizing and humbling. That night was also the first night we made love.

"Sit down, Essie," he said. He paced the room and his power filled it. I sat quietly and waited.

"Hank, I…"

"You what, Essie?"

"Nothing," I murmured.

"You're sitting right in front of me, but you're still running. If you want me, Essie, you'll have to fight for me." He crossed his arms over his chest and watched me.

"Will you still fight for me?" I whispered, afraid of his answer.

"I have fought for you from the moment I laid eyes on you...and I never stopped. Not for one moment."

He was right and it made my shame more debilitating. The silence was heavy and my brain was jumbled.

"Do you still love me?" he asked calmly.

I glanced up and my eyes locked with his. Having nothing left to lose, I nodded my head yes.

"Then you need to show me."

"I don't know how." I was stricken. How could I erase a year of pain and anger?

"Essie, when you left me you were still a girl. I didn't realize it—I was too close. You became your own woman this year. As much as it sickens me that we weren't together when this happened, maybe this was the way it was supposed to be."

"You watched me. You saw everything I did. Why didn't you drag me home?" I asked. He wasn't prone to rash action, but he did have the wild possessive streak of a Were.

"Trust me, I was tempted...but I wanted you to grow, and because I had Dwayne's ear and big mouth I felt secure. Not to mention your Granny said, and I quote 'I will rip your alpha ass apart if you don't let that girl find herself'."

God, my Granny loved me something fierce. Standing up to your alpha was serious business. "What did Dwayne tell you?" I asked as I felt my cheeks heat.

"You'll have to ask him." He gave me a half smirk that made me want to weep with joy and tackle him to the ground at the same time.

We stared at each other for a long time. I literally ached to touch him, but I still wasn't sure what the ground rules were. Did I have to pay penance? I was willing to do anything to regain his trust.

"You're going to have to make the first move, Essie," he said quietly and leaned back against the wall.

He was right and I was scared. Maybe he and Granny were correct. Maybe I did have to grow up. I was no longer just the alpha's gal pal. I was my own woman—an agent, a strong, whole person.

His green eyes turned a silvery blue and I felt wanted for exactly who I was—the crazy girl who would continue to attract trouble and make mistakes. The one who could love him like no other and the one who could finally accept his love in return.

I stood slowly and slipped the straps of my sundress off my shoulders. His body tensed, but he stayed still. I let it fall to the floor and I giggled.

"I'm still wired." I grinned and approached him. My insides danced wildly and the scent of cinnamon filled the room. I was wearing a bra, panties, kick ass wedge Pradas *that belonged to Dwayne*, a wire and a small gun strapped to my inner thigh. I had never felt sexier in my life.

"Officer, I'm going to have to ask you to remove your weapon," Hank said in his *sheriff's voice*.

"Wait, isn't that my line? I'm the agent," I answered as I bit back a laugh.

"True, but I'm the sheriff...and your alpha. I trump. Remove the gun. I plan to spend some time there and I prefer to keep my manly parts."

"I prefer that you keep your manly parts too," I said and stopped a breath away from him. His body went as tight as a drum and his Mr. Happy was very happy. I knew it took everything he had not to lunge at me. I marveled at his control and quite honestly at mine too.

Carefully, I unstrapped my gun and put it on the coffee table. "Will you help me with the wire?"

"Please?" His lopsided grin melted my insides.

"Please," I whispered.

Having tape pulled from one's body was not the usual foreplay I was used to with Hank, but it rocked my world at the moment. He ran his fingertips gently over the reddened skin and followed it with his lips. Somehow my bra and panties disappeared too. How had I not noticed that? Wait, who the hell cared?

I stood before him in only my borrowed heels, feeling shy yet sexy. "You're a little overdressed," I murmured as

I slid my hands under his shirt and pushed it up over his broad and familiar chest. The light sprinkling of dark hair tickled my fingers and the growl low in his throat made me grab onto him for balance.

He did nothing to help me as I pushed the material over his head. The only clue that he wasn't as in control as he pretended to be was his heart. It beat rapidly in his chest and his breathing was labored.

With shaking hands, I undid his belt and eased his jeans to the floor. He kicked off his shoes and stepped out of his jeans. Clad only in tight gray boxer briefs, there was no denying he was as attracted to me as I was to him.

"Am I supposed to do everything?" I asked, unsure of how to play.

He put his arms up and locked his fingers behind his head. "I can't guarantee that I'll stand still much longer...but for the moment, I'm finding this interesting." His voice was husky and it sent tingles to my dancing insides.

"*Interesting*?" I rolled my eyes and decided interesting was for textbooks, not seductions. I clearly needed to amp up the action.

I quickly grabbed the elastic of his boxer briefs and pushed them down. Coming face to face with one of my favorite parts of his body, I gave it a kiss and was rewarded with a harsh intake of breath. I refused to be interesting...

"Essie," he warned. "I won't promise to be gentle. I want you too badly."

His arm muscles bulged and I could tell it took all he had to keep them locked behind his head. My heart pounded hard in my chest and I realized this was the first time I'd ever taken the lead and I liked it.

"I don't want gentle," I purred. "But if you move your hands, I'll get dressed and leave."

His eyes flashed. His wolf was so close to the surface, I almost took back my threat. However, my inner wolf was so excited I borrowed her confidence and continued.

"Go to the couch and sit," I instructed and waited to see what he'd do.

"Yes, ma'am." His grin was so evilly sexy I almost knocked him to the floor and yelled "Game over." But I held on and followed him.

He was such a beautiful man. My breath caught in my throat as my eyes roamed every inch of his body. I felt alive, sexy, naughty and very, very happy. Crawling on top of him, I straddled his legs carefully, making sure no lady parts touched any man parts. His moan unfurled a hot coil of lust low in my belly and I was unsure how much longer I could tease him.

Leaning forward, I traced his closed lips with the tip of my tongue. He tasted of man and sin. I coaxed his lips open and slowly explored his mouth. My eyes fluttered shut and my body clenched in anticipation of what I knew would happen...of what I wanted and needed to happen.

"No more," he ground out as his strong arms trapped my body against his, crushing my breasts to his chest and my pelvis to his. "Open your eyes, Essie. See me. See what you do to me," he demanded.

I opened my eyes and forgot how to breathe. His desire was overwhelming and matched the fire that was building inside of me. I had never wanted him more. His fingers found the spot that made speech impossible. I ground against his hand and whimpered my need. His lips captured my nipple and I arched, offering myself to him— mind, body and soul.

"I can't wait," he hissed as his fangs scraped my breast, sending chills rippling over my body.

"No waiting," I gasped and I took him in my hand. He was perfect, so hard and as smooth as silk. His hands grasped my hips in an unbreakable hold as he moved me where he wanted me.

"Put me inside you," he muttered hoarsely. His eyes were unfocused and he was close to snapping. The power I wielded over him made me bold and fearless. I guided him to me and eased my body onto his. My breath caught and I bit down on my lip as he stretched me to accommodate his girth. It was like coming home. The slight burn was painfully addictive and my body clenched in protest.

"Relax, baby," he whispered in my ear. "Let me in."

I teetered on the edge between pleasure and pain which excited me like nothing else. I slowly let my body accept his. Sheer excitement took the non-stop train through me as I hissed and cried out. The fit was so very tight and so very perfect. He was going to own my body and heart in the most intimate way.

The time for slow and easy had passed and his grip on my hips tightened as he moved my body up and down the thick length of him. Pleasure jolted through me as he took my nipple in his hot mouth. I contracted around his body and he swore, explaining in graphic detail what he wanted to do to me. The blood roaring in my ears made the sound of his voice a distant noise. A fullness overwhelmed me and I rocked in a sensual rhythm that was natural and age old.

"Oh my god," I moaned. "Too much." The sensitivity was intense and I didn't know how much more I could handle before I detonated.

"You're mine," he insisted. "Say it."

"You're mine too," I shot back.

"Say it, Essie," he demanded as he increased the speed to something that would have killed a mere human. We made love like the animals that we were. The sound of our bodies rapidly joining almost sent me over the edge.

"Mine," he growled. "Always."

"I'm yours," I screamed as colors ripped across my vision and my body gripped his like a vise. "Always." Tremors shook me violently as he continued his assault.

Hank went crazy and branded my body with his need. He threw back his head and howled as he joined me in climax.

We'd had sex many times, but it had never been like this. I'd be damned if I could remember my name, much less what year it was. I shook like a leaf as I came down from the most intense orgasm of my life. He pressed soft kisses all over my face and neck as I held on to the man I loved for dear life.

It had been more than sex…we had combined who we were and became a different entity altogether. Was this what it felt like to mate? Was he my true mate?

Shockingly a need tore through me again, but it was different. My body was useless, but my desire to be even closer to him bordered on obsession.

"What's happening to me?" I asked. I was lightheaded and my fangs had descended. All I could focus on was the tanned beautiful skin on his neck.

"Are you ready for this?" he asked as he held me at arm's length. "There's no going back."

"Wait. What?"

"Essie." He eased me off of him and walked in all his naked glory to the other side of the room. His body was taut and the veins in his muscles strained against his skin. "Our wolves want to mate. Is your human side willing to do that?" His gaze narrowed and I knew the internal battle he fought to have pushed me away. I felt it too.

He was asking me to become his. Forever. It was a silly question and I smiled. I had always wanted that. Maybe I hadn't been ready until this moment, but there was no doubt in my mind or heart whatsoever.

"Will you be mine—just mine?" I questioned him.

"I already am," he replied.

"I think I wanna bite you." I grinned and held my arms out.

"Think?"

"I know. I know I wanna bite you. Sink my teeth into you and take you off the market for the rest of your ridiculously long life."

He was on me so fast my head spun and I shrieked with laughter as he tickled me and held me close.

"I am so in love with you I can't see straight," he muttered against the skin on my neck.

"Me too. How do we do this? Will it hurt?"

"Considering I've never done it, I can't really answer that one. Although the stories say it causes the most intense orgasm one can have."

"Oh my hell," I whispered as my exhausted body miraculously came back to life. "We might die from it."

"True, but I'm willing to go down for such a noble cause." He grinned and my tummy did a somersault.

"On three?" I said in an unsteady voice.

He nodded. His eyes were a silver blue and I knew mine matched. My body trembled and I was surprised to note his hands were shaky. I was scared, but had never felt so sure of anything in my life.

"One. Two. Three."

Holy Hell on a stick. He was right and then some.

It was surreal. It felt like a movie, but it was my life—my choice. Our choice. With our eyes locked our fangs dropped. My gums burned with need, but my overheated body moved in slow motion. My mind swirled with both fear and anticipation. Not knowing what to expect was as alarming as it was exhilarating. The feral look in his eyes made every nerve in my body stand on end.

All of my senses were sharper and they were trained on Hank—his scent especially. My nipples beaded painfully and the sensual ache between my thighs made me dizzy. His fangs grazed the skin on my neck and I shuddered. His breathing was labored and the evidence of his arousal was pressed against my stomach as my hands roamed his body desperately.

Stark need—naked desire. I had never wanted anyone or anything like I wanted Hank. It was more than want or even need. It was simply necessary. The compulsion to crawl inside him was overwhelming. Our wolves were so close to the surface, I worried we'd shift, but no. We didn't shift. We became something more.

His fangs pierced the soft skin of my neck as my own plunged into his shoulder. The burn went from painful to pleasurable almost immediately. I shrieked at the invasion and came so hard I sobbed. His body shook and he held me tight as we performed the ritual that bound us together for eternity. He touched a place so deep inside of me, I never wanted him to leave. I was unsure of how much time had passed. It could have been hours or minutes. The closeness I now felt trumped what I had felt before and it awed me. Running my hands over his face and tangling my fingers in his thick hair I pulled his mouth to mine and I was complete. It was done. We lived through it...*barely*...and we now belonged to each other. Rolling me beneath him, Hank entered my body with infinite tenderness.

Our lovemaking was slow this time and his eyes stayed locked on mine. I could swear he was looking into my soul. Tears fell from my eyes as I moved in a rhythm with my mate that sealed our bond.

"I love you," I whispered. "Forever."

"I love you more," he said as his hips began to move faster and he plunged deeper into my very willing body.

"Not possible," I shot back as little shocks of pleasure rolled through me. I jerked and undulated beneath him as I cried out.

The gentle lovemaking came to an end as we were consumed with what I could only call mating frenzy— nothing was off limits and it was impossible to be close enough. However, we tried and tried and tried until we succeeded. We were now completely spent or dead. I wasn't sure which...

"I'm pretty sure I died," I moaned as I tried to lift my head.

"If this is dead, I'm all in," Hank said as his hands continued to memorize my body.

"That was amazing," I murmured as the feeling in my limbs slowly came back. "Will it be that way every time?" I asked. Part of me hoped he would say yes, but the other part of me was sure I wouldn't live through that again.

"From what I understand, it gets even better. We'll just have to put in a lot of practice and find out." He grinned and I felt it in my toes. "We do have a few more rooms to christen in this house..."

I bolted upright as reality sunk in. "Oh my god, Hank, what about my job and stuff? We kind of forgot to discuss the logistics." I realized I didn't really care about my job at the moment, but we should have some kind of plan.

"We'll deal with that later. We have a mission here and the rest will work itself out," he said as he lifted me and took me to our bed.

"I'm exhausted," I muttered as I tried to keep my eyes open.

"Go to sleep," he whispered in my ear. He wrapped his huge hard body around my smaller, softer one and I smiled sleepily.

"Don't leave me," I pleaded as I slipped into sleep.

"I will never leave you, Essie. Never."

Chapter 10

"Well, I'll be damned," Junior shouted joyfully from the door of our bedroom. "It's about time."

I shrieked and yanked the sheet up over my naked body. It was one thing to be naked for a shift with the Pack. It was another thing altogether to be naked after a sex-a-thon in front of my mate's brother.

"Out," Hank bellowed. "And erase the image of Essie from your brain or I'll beat it out of you."

"No prob, baby bro-bro, but you need to get your mated asses out here. We have a situation." He grinned, winked and left the room.

"How does he know we're mated?" I asked as I grabbed my sundress and yanked it on.

"Scent. It'd be pretty hard to miss." Hank smiled like a cat who'd eaten a canary and I punched him in the shoulder. "Ouch," he grunted.

"That didn't hurt." I rolled my eyes and attempted to hold back my smile. "You are just full of yourself."

"I am a very happy man." He grabbed me and planted a big one on my willing lips. My head spun and I seriously considered making Junior wait while I exercised my new conjugal rights with my mate, but I knew he'd just barge back in.

"Come on, happy man, Junior's got some intel."

Hand in hand we went out to face the real world again.

The den was a wreck and Junior was taking it in with glee. My panties and bra were on the lamp and Hank's boxer briefs were hanging off the ceiling fan... *How did that happen?* I quickly ran around the room and gathered all the incriminating evidence as Junior chuckled and Hank strutted around like a peacock.

"Okay," I huffed in my professional voice and tried to pretend I hadn't just shoved my panties in my purse. "What's going on?"

"First of all, I want to say welcome to the family. I love you. Definitely not in the way Hank does, but like a sister. I am relieved to know that someone who could shoot my balls off while blindfolded is part of my family."

"Um...thank you, I think," I said as I shook my head and grinned.

Hank tossed me a bottle of water and we all sat down at the kitchen table.

"Out with it," Hank told Junior. "Oh, and we have some prints to run on Puck Flame."

"It's the self tanner," Junior said.

"I'm sorry, what?" I asked.

"The self tanner. I went to the agency to make sure Tina #1 wasn't dead, which unfortunately she wasn't, and I bought some of the stinky self tanner." He stared at us like we should understand what he meant.

"What are you talking about?" Hank demanded.

"Oh right, I get ahead of myself," Junior muttered. "The self tanner eliminates scent. It's why we couldn't track the girls who were abducted. It's a compound with a combination of chemicals I don't know."

"That's impossible," Hank said.

"I thought so too, but I can't identify them."

"Junior, there is no way you are unable to identify a compound," Hank argued. Junior shrugged and stared at the table.

"Color me confused, but why in the heck would you think Junior could discern a chemical compound? No offense, Junior," I said.

"None taken," he muttered.

"Do you wanna tell her?" Hank asked his brother.

"Nope."

76

"Then I will," he threatened.

"You promised," Junior whined.

"Junior, Essie is my mate and soon to be my wife. She..."

"Wait. When did you ask me to marry you?" I demanded. "Did I miss something? Did you put a ring on my finger?"

"No." Hank smacked his forehead and blew out an exasperated breath. "It's common sense that we'll get married. We live amongst humans and they'll expect it before I knock you up."

"Oh My God!" I screamed. "You just lost some major panty privileges. You need to ask me to marry you on your freakin' knees and I want a big ring that's not cubic zirconia. It needs to be romantic and it needs to be a surprise. Do you understand me?"

"Um...yes," he said as he bit back a grin. "I understand."

"She's gonna be one hell of an alpha partner." Junior laughed and stood to leave.

"Sit," Hank snapped. "You think I'd forget what we were talking about because I got my balls handed to me?"

"I was hoping so," he mumbled.

"You tell her or I will."

Junior sat silently and gave his brother the stink eye.

"Somebody tell me," I insisted as I stood up. "Also, Mr. Wolfboy, we are not having kids any time soon."

"Got it." He grinned and slapped my ass. Why the hell his Neanderthal behavior was a turn on was a mystery to me.

"My brother holds a masters in biochemical engineering, speaks four languages fluently and has a doctorate in engineering."

I was stunned to silence. My voice literally wouldn't work.

"This is exactly why I don't want anyone knowing this," Junior ground out angrily. "My stud factor drops dramatically when chicks find out I'm a nerd."

"You're brilliant?" I asked, still in shock.

"He's off the charts for MENSA," Hank added as Junior shot him a death glare.

"Are you freakin' kidding me?" I yelled. "Junior, that is the hottest thing I've ever heard. Someone who looks like you with brains? Oh my god, the chicks will be begging you to mate with them. In fact, I hope you're using condoms because once this gets out the entire Pack of single gals plus all the Weres in the surrounding states are going to try to trap your butt into marriage."

"Really?" he asked doubtfully.

Hank was looking a little put out at my excitement over his brother and I giggled. "Don't worry, baby," I cooed. "You have all the attributes I need."

"You think this will help me get more babes?" Junior mulled this new information over.

For as brilliant as he apparently was, he was still a lazy, skirt-chasing good 'ole boy.

"Yes, you will get more babes," Hank added dryly. "Enough about that — get back to why you can't figure the chemical compound out."

"It flummoxed me. I recognize some of it, but it seems to mutate genetically. It's quite brilliant and whoever is making it is loaded."

"Do you think the Council is behind this?" I asked.

"Doubtful," Hank answered. "Why would they be kidnapping their own? And what would they be doing with them?"

"Only one way to find out," I muttered and pulled the offending bottle from my purse.

"I was wondering if you had any panties in your purse?" Junior asked as he laughed heartily at his own joke.

"That's funny," I shot back. "I was wondering if I could use your nuts for target practice."

He shut up fast.

"I don't like this, Essie," Hank said tersely. "Not one bit."

"Don't, Hank," I warned. "I love you, but that doesn't change what I do or who I am."

He sat silently and fumed.

"Oh, two of those agency humans called and want a meeting with Hank at ten tomorrow," Junior told us. "They want to meet in the sheriff's office."

"That's when I'm supposed to be at the agency. Which ones want the meeting?" I asked.

"Peter Pyre and Paul Tinder." All three of us snickered at the ridiculous names.

"They're supposed to be off on assignment with some models. The timing is awfully convenient," I muttered.

"The timing is planned," Hank cut me off. "They'll keep me busy while they try to take you."

"Getting the alpha's mate would be a coup," Junior added.

"No one but you knows we're mated," I reasoned. "And why would it make any difference if they had the alpha's mate? We don't even know what they're doing with the girls."

"I can tell you this. If they're smart enough to create a tanning compound that erases scent they aren't just killing our girls. I would bet they're alive and being experimented on." Junior ran his hands through his hair and sighed unhappily.

My stomach roiled. Junior had a good point, but who was doing this? The three idiot humans?

Hank was pissed. He pulled a knife and a small transmitter out of a kitchen drawer. "Essie, this will hurt, but you'll heal quickly. You can't wear a wire or you'll get busted so I'm going to put a device in your arm that will let us track you."

"Where did you get that? We don't have those at WTF." It was tiny. I thought we had state of the art everything at WTF, but I was clearly mistaken.

Junior raised his hand bashfully. "I invented it. My litter of kittens kept running off and I was sick and tired of searching for them so I made a tiny tracking device."

I stopped short of commenting on the fact that Junior owned a litter of kittens. I was far too grateful that they would be able to follow my movement.

I extended my arm and shut my eyes. "Cut away."

"He's going to need to place it where you have some body fat," Junior said. "I'd suggest her ass."

Hank growled and I sputtered. "You think my ass is fat?"

"No." Junior turned bright red. "You have a lovely ass," he quickly said as Hank's growl grew louder. "Women have more fat in their asses and boobs. He could also place it in your boob, but you have really nice ones and…I'm gonna stop now before I die a violent death."

"Good thinking," Hank snapped as he turned me around and stabbed me in the butt.

"Owwww," I grunted. "A little warning?"

"It's better this way. Anticipation sucks." He inserted the device and put a butterfly bandage over it. "It will heal in an hour. Shouldn't even leave a mark."

I was a bit grumpy from being stabbed in the butt so I sucked back my water to keep from calling my mate nasty names. I was happy they would be able to find me no matter where I was, but the implementation was lacking.

"So here's the deal. I'll meet with the humans. Essie will go as planned to the agency, and Junior, you will tail her if they leave with her. Essie, you will be armed. I would assume that wherever they take you will lead us to the missing girls. Use the tanner, but let Dwayne sniff you tonight so he can pick up your trail if needed. Everyone clear?"

We nodded. It was as solid of a plan as we could have at the moment.

"How do you know about Dwayne's smelling talent?" I asked.

"Trust me, I know more about Dwayne than I ever wanted to." Hank grinned ruefully.

"Oh my god," I squealed. "Does he have secrets I don't know about?"

"He's a three hundred year old Vampyre. He has secrets none of us know about."

"Speaking of," I said. "We need to go tell Granny and Dwayne the good news."

Hank smiled and grabbed my hand. "Lead on, my mate. Lead on."

Chapter 11

"Honey, I'm so happy for you." Granny trapped me in a hug that made me gasp for air.

"Thanks," I choked out as I extricated myself.

"I know you're my alpha," she warned Hank with a twinkle in her eye, "but I will tear you a new butt if you hurt my girl."

"Duly noted." Hank laughed.

"Will there be a wedding?" Dwayne asked as he bounced with excitement.

Hank blanched and quickly stepped away from me.

"Apparently, but he hasn't asked me properly yet. However, in the event he gets his act together and does it right, I would like Granny to give me away and I want Dwayne to be my maid, or um, man of honor."

"Yessssssssssss," Dwayne squealed and hugged me harder than Granny did. "Can I wear a dress?"

"Well…um, sure." I was certain I would live to regret that answer.

"Oh my goodness gracious," he muttered distractedly. "We have so much to do—dresses, invites, showers…Wait. What is that funky smell?"

"Self tanner," I told him. "What do you smell?"

He circled me and sniffed the air. "Well, if that's not the damndest thing. It's muted your Were smell—almost eliminates it."

"But you can still smell me?" He was amazing.

"Yep, but you're stinky."

"I can't smell her Were at all," Granny said. "What the hell is in that? Did Junior take a look at it?"

"You know about Junior's brains?" I asked, shocked.

"Baby girl, Granny knows all," she said. "Did he examine it?"

I nodded. "He can't tell what's in it."

She was surprised, but I was more so. What else about this town didn't I know? Shifter strip clubs, drag clubs, Junior was smarter than Einstein...

"I put a tracker in Essie. She'll go to the agency as planned, but I want you two at the station on standby in case this gets as ugly as I think it will," Hank explained. "Dwayne, can you shoot a gun?"

Dwayne rolled his eyes. "Hanky-poo, Dwayne doesn't need a gun. I have crap in my repertoire that will make you lose sleep for the rest of your life."

We all digested that nugget silently for a moment and then moved on. If Dwayne wanted us to know exactly what he was capable of, he would have volunteered it. Part of me hoped I would never have to find out, but the other half was dying to know.

"Speaking of secrets, what did you tell Hank about me?"

"You mean *Jeff*. What did I tell *Jeff* about you? If I had known it was Hank I wouldn't have told him anything. You're my BFF and I would shred someone's skin from their body and shove their bones down their dead ass throat for you."

"That's really sweet," I muttered, trying not to picture that. "What was it that you told *Jeff*?"

Dwayne huffed a huge and dramatic sigh. Hank had the decency to look a bit ashamed and I waited...

"As you know, Essie, we had lots and lots of super fun slumber parties," Dwayne began and I nodded. "Well, you tend to talk and cry in your sleep."

"No, I don't."

"How would you know? You're asleep," Granny added her two cents. "And he's right. You kept me awake for two years straight during high school."

"Fine. I talk. I cry. What the hell did I say?"

"You called out for Hank every time I stayed over. It broke my heart, even though I don't technically have one. I would just hold you and rock you till you stopped and fell back into a deep sleep."

I didn't have a smart-ass come back. I wasn't embarrassed or uncomfortable. I was just quiet. The feeling of Hank's hands on my back felt safe and right. When Dwayne added his bald head to my shoulder and Granny took my hand in hers, my world sat squarely on its axis and I knew whatever journey I had chosen had led me back to where I was supposed to be. Tomorrow would be a new day filled with uncertainty and very possibly danger, but right now all was right with my world.

"Come on, baby. Let's go home," Hank said.

"Will you guys be okay?" I asked my granny and BFF.

"Oh, hell yeah. We're gonna play Twister and then try on wigs and girdles," Granny informed us.

Hank seemed confused, so I pushed him out the door before he asked questions he didn't want the answers to.

"That visual was disturbing," he said as we climbed on the motorcycle.

"Yep," I agreed. "Do you think we can go home and you can put some new visuals in my head?" I grabbed his perfect butt and squeezed.

He chuckled and pulled me forward for a toe-curling kiss. "I do believe that can be arranged."

***

The morning dawned bright and sunny. The familiar sweet smell of the ocean breeze was comforting, but even that and the memory of a night full of aerobic sex with Hank couldn't erase the sense of impending doom that had settled in the pit of my stomach. There were too many unanswered questions. The humans were the wild card.

A block away from the agency, I hunkered down in my little car and wracked my brain for clues we had missed. The humans, if they had developed the self-tanning lotion, were brilliant and rich. I was convinced they knew about Shifters, which was highly unusual. They were the key...abducting Weres...erasing scents...possibly experimenting…Wait. Erasing scents. That was it. Could it be that simple?

I quickly texted Dwayne and told him to go buy some self tanner and then meet me at my car in ten minutes. I gave him no other directions. If I needed to send him back in I would, but I had a feeling I wouldn't have to. It was 9:35. I was due at the agency in twenty-five minutes. There was plenty of time for some quick recon. If I was right, this was huge. However, if I was right, Hank would forbid me to go in.

Waiting in my car, I heard familiar nasal laughter. My gut clenched and my claws itched to come out and play. Slowly I eased the car window down and ducked low in my seat.

"I hope they take her today," Tina #1 growled. "After they're done with her and the rest of them, they'll kill them."

"Agreed. There's simply not enough oxygen for losers like Essie McGee in this world." Tina #2 laughed.

"Wait. Are you serious?" Tina #3 demanded.

"About what?" Tina #2 asked.

"The oxygen thingie."

"I will pretend you didn't say that, moron."

"You don't have to be a bitch," Tina #3 hissed. "I could kill you so easily."

"Like to see you try. Anyway, once she's dead, I'll get Hank for keeps," Tina #2 purred.

"Why do you get him?" Tina #1 whined.

"Because I called him first. You two idiots can share the fire boys when this is over."

"I just hope it's over soon. None of us have gotten laid in a year," Tina #2 muttered with disgust.

"Keep your voice down. No one needs to know our business," Tina #3 shot back menacingly. "Once the fire boys complete the experiment they promised they would be all ours. In fact, Hank can screw himself. I like my guys hot."

As their laughter died away, I sat bolt upright in my seat. Junior was correct, the humans were experimenting on the Weres. That was sick and what in the hell was the experiment? Why did the Tina's call them fire boys? Were those their stupid fake names or were they something more? How did the Weres let the humans take them? We could overpower a human with our eyes closed…Were the humans working for another species of Were and kidnapping wolves?

My need to walk into the agency and tear the limbs off of the humans, or whatever the hell they were, and the Tinas was overwhelming, but that would be a grave mistake. I needed them to take me to where the girls were hidden. If I killed the messenger, I'd lose the prize.

"Dragons," Dwayne whispered into my cracked window.

"Oh my god," I shrieked. "You scared me to death."

He grinned and slipped into the back seat. "You look alive to me."

"Why are you in the back?" I asked.

"I've seen this in the movies," he explained. "No one will actually know we're having a conversation. They'll think you're my driver and pass right on by."

Deciding not to touch that theory, I waited for him to continue.

"They're not human. They're Dragons."

"*What?*" I hissed.

"I said they're not hum…"

"I heard you. Are you sure?" My skin felt tight on my body and I prayed he was mistaken. This was far worse than I ever could have imagined. I thought maybe they were wolves from a rival Pack and they'd used the self tanner to disguise their scent and possibly blackmail our Pack into paying ransom…

"This is not very good, Essie." Dwayne fretted in the back seat.

He was right. My brain was on overload. They were rich, smart, dangerous and seriously hard to kill. They had clearly duped the Council and now they were using science to do god knows what with my Pack.

"Listen to me," I snapped, formulating a plan as it fell from my lips. "I am going in and I'm going to let them take me to the other girls. You are going to the sheriff's office and when his meeting with the assholes is over you will tell Hank what you told me. Detain the Dragons if you can.

85

I'll be safer with only one Dragon and three, soon-to-be-dead, traitorous she-wolves. Let him know the Tinas are involved and the Dragons are experimenting on our wolves. Tell him if he tries to stop me from going to the girls he'll be signing their death warrant. He has to trust me and let me do my job. Do you understand me?" I sucked in a huge breath as I'd not taken in a lick of air during my diatribe.

"Can I ask you something weird?" Dwayne inquired.

"Does it pertain?"

"Yes."

"Fine, but hurry. I'm due in the agency in ten."

"Don't speak till I finish," Dwayne said in a weary voice I'd never heard. "I am going to bite you. I will drink a very small amount of your blood so I can track you definitively. I don't trust my sense of smell enough where your life is concerned. You will then bite me and drink. You will find it disgusting, disturbing and possibly somewhat erotic, which is gross because you're straight and I'm gay, but you will do it. My blood will give you vampire strength. It's temporary, so don't freak. Let's do it."

"Was all that a joke?" I stammered.

"What? The straight and gay part?" He was confused. "Or the temporary part?"

"All of it," I yelled.

"None of it's a joke, Essie. We don't have a lot of time here, so I'd suggest you slap your fangs onto my neck and suck."

"This is the craziest thing I've ever thought about doing," I muttered as Dwayne crawled over the seat and settled himself next to me.

"No crazier than going after Dragons," he countered.

I rolled my eyes and reluctantly let my fangs descend. "What super powers will this give me? Will I be able to fly?"

Dwayne grinned and shrugged. "You'd have to pretty much drain me to get that skill."

"Shut the hell up! You can fly? You never told me that." Color me very impressed.

"You never asked. Give me your wrist and you take my neck."

"Will this hurt you?" I asked as I leaned in.

"Don't know. Never let a wolf near my neck." He grinned and gave me a quick hug. "I love you, Essie. Before you came into my life, I had considered ending myself. Three hundred years is a long time to be alone. You've given me hope, a career as a drag queen and a dysfunctional family. I am supremely grateful. Bite me."

And because I trusted him…I did.

It was odd and kind of icky. Not erotic for me at all and from the way Dwayne was laughing, I figured it wasn't a turn-on for him either. He bit my wrist as I swallowed down his blood that tasted bizarrely like mac and cheese. After taking a quick nip of my O positive he closed the wound with his tongue.

I withdrew my fangs and closed my eyes as a rush of heat blasted through me, ending at my toes and fingertips. My vision sharpened and my sense of smell was insane. Holy hell, the self tanner smelled like butt.

"You have to go," Dwayne said as he gently pushed me out of the car. "Remember, you are not superhuman. You're just stronger with heightened senses for a day or two or three…"

"You have no clue how long this will last, do you?" I asked dryly.

"Um…no, but I don't regret it for a moment. You needed it and I gave it. Ohhh, and that wasn't at all sexy. It tickled and felt squishy."

"Thanks," I muttered as I grabbed my overnight bag and checked my gun.

"Are your panties up your ass?" Dwayne asked, concerned.

"No. Why?"

"Well, it looked like you were adjusting your hoohoo and I figured…"

"Dwayne," I hissed. "I was not adjusting my *hoohoo*. I was checking my gun, which I wear on the inside of my thigh, but thank you for your concern."

"Welcome."

I studied him silently for a moment. He was three hundred. Maybe he knew something I didn't. "Dwayne, do you know how to kill a Dragon?"

He nodded in reply, not smiling at all. "The usual. Take the heart out, or decapitate him, but that's a bit difficult with all those sharp scales."

"Right." So much for another way to off a Dragon.

"I plan to mind meld those jack-offs at the Sherriff's office," he informed me smugly.

"I thought that kind of thing only worked on humans."

"Maybe. I've never tried it on Dragons, but I can't wait." He clapped his hands like a child on Christmas morning and I gave him the eyeball.

"You will be careful," I told him. "If you get hurt, I will kick your ass."

I walked away as his eyes filled with happy tears. Dwayne was a piece of work, but he was my piece of work and I was going to keep him.

Chapter 12

"Did you use the self tanner, dear?" Puck the Schmuck inquired. Of course he knew I had used it because he was a freakin' Dragon. His nose was as good or better than mine.

I nodded and smiled coyly as I listened for the Tinas. Where were they? "I did. I used it all over, Pucky—just like you instructed."

"Wonderful." He stared at me like I was a tasty piece of meat and an alarming thought burst through my head. Are wolves a tasty treat for Dragons? Are they fattening up the girls so they can eat them? It seemed a lot of trouble to go to just to eat wolves, but Dragons were weird.

"What are we doing today? More pictures?" I asked as I dropped my overnight bag on the floor at my feet. It landed with a loud thud in the quiet office.

"No, no, sweet girl. I have thrilling news for you. I scanned the Polaroids we took yesterday and sent them to New York. You have booked a major magazine spread." He leered at me and it took everything I had to feign excitement.

"Oh my god," I gushed and fanned myself. "What magazine?"

He was typing quickly into his phone, a slight smile played on his lips.

"I'm sorry, what?" he asked as he pocketed his phone.

"What magazine?" I repeated.

He stared at me blankly for a moment and then recovered. "Oh, yes...*Glamour. Glamour Magazine.*"

I squealed with glee as the bastard laughed and stared straight at my chest. I smelled the Tinas before I saw them. It all happened so fast I was shocked. He had clearly just texted them and I got blindsided. I felt the needle pierce the skin on the back of my neck and the burning substance enter my body. The Tinas watched with rabid pleasure as my body hit the floor. I was furious that I had left myself open for an attack from behind. That was 101 and Hank was going to kill me if the Dragons didn't do the job first.

"That will knock a wolf out for days," Tina #1 hissed.

"How much did you use?" Puck demanded angrily. Tina blanched and backed away.

"Just a little more than usual," she said. "She's strong. We wouldn't want her to wake up and ruin everything."

Puck seemed mollified and watched me sink into lala land. I closed my eyes and waited for the darkness to come, but it didn't. *What was going on?*

"She's out," he said. "Let's go."

But I wasn't... The shot they gave me might have knocked out a Werewolf, but it did nothing to a Vampyre. Keeping my eyes closed and my body slack, I mentally gave Dwayne the biggest kiss and hug imaginable. I was going to live and I was going to take no prisoners.

The Tinas dragged me through the office and dumped me into the trunk of a car, banging my head on as many hard surfaces as they could find. They laughed and congratulated themselves on the impending end of my life. It took an enormous amount of restraint on my part not to kill them dead. I consoled myself that there would be time enough for killing them very soon.

The ride was short and I knew we hadn't crossed the bridge back to the mainland. The scent of the ocean was in the distance, so we had clearly driven inland. I was surprised and greatly relieved they were keeping the girls in Hung. It occurred to me there might be more Dragons involved than the three we knew about, but Dragons were an egotistical bunch. I was hedging my bets that whatever they were doing, they wanted full credit for it and they were working rogue.

The car stopped and I was yanked from the trunk. The lovely Tinas dragged my body across a rock-strewn path and I chanced a peek. We were at an old deserted resort. It had been abandoned when I was a child. A cult from out West had owned the place and a drug bust turned shootout had occurred here. About ten local human police officers had died in that raid and most of the cult. No one wanted the place and no one ever came out here.

"Put her in the holding area with the others," Puck said in a clipped and furious voice. "And if you killed her with an overdose, I will rip your limbs from your body and feed them to you."

The Tinas were silent and far more careful with my limp body than they had been. I mentally calculated if Hank and the gang were on their way yet.

I was sure Junior had followed in his wolf form. A car would have been spotted and no one had said anything. I sniffed the air, but couldn't detect his scent. *Where was he*? I was good, but I was fairly sure I would have a hard time taking out a Dragon and three wolves alone while trying to rescue the girls.

"Drop her. He can't see us anymore," Tina #1 snapped. My body was dumped on the floor and a swift and hard kick to my stomach followed. I swallowed my grunt of pain and took everything they handed out as if I were already dead.

"It was your idea to give her enough to send her into a coma, shit for brains," Tina #2 growled. "If anyone dies because of this, it's you."

"Shut up," Tina #1 said. "No one dies today except the prisoners and this bitch."

"How do you know that?" Tina #3 asked.

"Because I just do."

The clack of their heels on the wooden floor as they exited was music to my ears. I lay still for a moment in case they came back.

"Is she dead?" a frightened voice whispered.

"I don't know," another answered.

"Oh god, it's Essie. Please let her be okay. Please," a third voice whispered brokenly.

91

I slowly raised my head and looked around the room to the gasps of the chained women. It had been a kitchen at one point. The remains of a sink and stove were sitting cockeyed against the decaying wall. The girls' arms and legs were bound with silver and they were chained to old rusty pipes that protruded from the walls. Mottled red skin and dried blood around the shackles proved they were bound with the offending metal. Silver prohibited shifting.

"Essie, it's me. Sandy Moongie. Are you okay?"

"Sandy?" That couldn't be Sandy Moongie, or if it was she'd lost half her body weight and turned into a supermodel. "You look fantastic."

"Um...thanks." She blushed and looked down. "Weight Watchers and pole dancing."

"Amazing." I grinned and gave her the thumbs up and then remembered we weren't exactly at a class reunion. Glancing around and listening for footsteps, I slowly got up. I was a little wobbly, but I was functional.

"I'm going to get you out of here," I told them and was greeted with quiet sobs. "What have they done to you?"

"They've injected us with something to make us ovulate at a rapid pace," Frankie Mac told me as she stifled her crying. Jenny Packer and Debbie Swink nodded in agreement.

What the hell was going on here?

"Dragon Puck is a doctor and they harvested our eggs," Sandy whispered. "They used no painkiller. We were awake the entire time. They plan to do it again today." She winced and curled in on herself.

This was barbaric, and if they were doing what I thought they were doing it was horrifying. Shifters could not cross breed. The results of crossbreeding in the past had resulted in tragic and unspeakable deaths for the mothers and babies. Had the Dragons figured out the secret? I almost threw up in my mouth.

"They're trying to create a super race. It's not just wolves. They've tried this with Panther Shifters and Bear Shifters," Debbie added, her pretty face as white as a sheet.

"Did it work?" I asked, trying to hold back my fury.

92

"No. They think the mistake was they actually impregnated the other women and had them try to carry the babies. They all died. Violently," Jenny said sadly.

"How do you know all this?" I asked as I silently made my way to them.

"The Dragons like to talk," Sandy spat with disgust. "Now they're going to try to incubate eggs and sperm outside of the body and grow a baby. They're convinced the failure stemmed from the mothers."

"They'll have a difficult time doing that if they're dead." I pulled on Sandy's chain and winced. Silver burned our skin, but that was just too damned bad at the moment. Time was of the essence and I had no clue where my back up was. Wait, part of the story was missing... "Why are they doing this?"

"They want to cause an upheaval with the Council—destroy it. Introduce a new breed that wouldn't be accepted and then petition for a new leadership," Debbie said. "They want to rule the world."

I shuddered at the thought and examined the chains.

"You can't break them," Sandy said. "We've tried."

"So little confidence," I muttered as I shook my head and sighed dramatically. "Who pulled the fire alarm six times in one day in the tenth grade?"

"You did." Jenny giggled.

"That's right. Who slipped a fake speech to that turdwaffle, Ted Head, at graduation?" I asked.

"You did," Sandy gasped and laughed. "I about died when he dropped the F bomb three times during his speech."

"So did the principal," Frankie added with glee.

"Who spiked the punch at prom?" I was getting into this.

"Actually, that was me," Debbie said.

"Oh, right. I forgot. Are you sure that wasn't me?"

"Quite sure." Debbie grinned happily. "I got suspended for it, but it was worth it."

"Okay fine, I regretfully can't take credit for that one, but I did do all that other stuff. Right?"

They nodded and looked at me like I was crazy. They were right and they were wrong. I was nuts, but I could also break the chains thanks to Dwayne.

"Hold tight, ladies. This may hurt since your skin is so raw, but if you can shift when I'm done, you'll heal."

Quickly and efficiently I yanked the chains from the wall much to their delighted shock. Removing the shackles was more difficult and I blanched at the pain I caused them, but their stoic bravery awed me. They made small grunts and whimpers, but no one cried out.

"You need to shift and run. I want you out of here quickly." I helped them to their feet and herded them towards the door.

"Essie, what about you? We're not leaving you here alone," Frankie Mac insisted as she came to an abrupt halt. The girls agreed and refused to move. Why in the world had I ever left this place? Loyalty like this was virtually impossible to find...

"Guys, while I was gone, I trained and became an agent for WTF. I work for the Council. I was sent down to find and rescue you."

"Are you back home to stay or are you leaving again?" Jenny asked.

"I don't know," I admitted and blushed. "But, um..."

"You mated with Hank!" Sandy squealed and gave me a hug. "I can smell it and I'm so happy. But even more important than that, you're our new female alpha," she added reverently and got down on her knees followed by my other friends. The air in the room swirled with magic and my skin heated. I froze and watched them. My inner wolf chuffed with pride, but my human side was torn. I didn't deserve this kind of worship. I hadn't earned it, but I could change that in the next hour...and I would.

"Get up," I whispered frantically. "I'm just Essie, the goof ball from high school. Don't bow to me."

The girls stood slowly but kept their heads bowed in respect.

"I'll bend you over and kiss your butt for saving my life," Frankie said as she lifted her grateful eyes to mine. "But the timing is wrong. Essie, you're right about us shifting to heal, but wrong about us leaving. We stay and fight. I don't care if you're WTF or WTH or WWW...you're Pack and Pack sticks together. Period."

I wanted to cry, but didn't have time. I knew no amount of begging or threatening would make them leave, so I had to formulate a plan.

"Okay, fine," I mumbled as I paced the room. "I'm armed and you're not. I also drank Vampyre blood, so I have super strength for a while."

"Oh my god," Sandy gasped, totally impressed. "Can you fly?"

I laughed and shook my head. "I wish. I want all of you to stay here and go back to where you were chained. Keep the chains near you, but don't let them touch your skin. You need to be able to shift at a moment's notice. It's dark enough in here that they won't notice you've been freed immediately."

"What are you going to do?" Jenny asked fearfully.

"What I've been trained to do," I answered her honestly without spelling everything out. "Will you gals be able to kill the Tinas if they come back?"

They stared at me like I'd grown an extra nose.

"Let me rephrase the question...if the Tinas try to kill you, which I guarantee they will, will you defend yourselves?"

"Do we actually have to kill them?" Debbie asked.

"Well, if you want to come out of here alive...I'd say yes." Maybe I should make them run. This was looking like a bloodbath in the making.

"I'll kill them dead and then I'll kill them again," Sandy said. "They've beaten the hell out of us on a daily basis for two weeks."

God, I liked Sandy.

"Wouldn't it be better if we held them and had them shunned?" Frankie suggested.

We all contemplated the ultimate punishment silently. Shunning was the most horrific thing that could happen to a Shifter. It was a fate worse than death. I mulled it over. Frankie did have a good point.

"I don't know." I hesitated. "I suppose if you can restrain them and get them chained up, we can leave their punishment to the Pack."

"I do vote for roughing them up a bit—maybe knocking out a few teeth," Jenny added hopefully.

I smiled at her enthusiasm. "I'm good with that as long as you also kick them in the stomach. Preferably till they vomit. Now, I have to go and see what's happening. Backup is on the way and we'll get you out of here soon."

"Essie, be careful," Sandy said. "We've missed you and it would just suck if you died today."

I grinned and gave her the thumbs up sign. "I have no plans to die today. I have too much to live for."

Chapter 13

Where in the world was my backup? I was actually going to try to do this one by the books, but the longer I waited the more danger the girls were in. If it was discovered they were out of their chains all hell would break loose. I sniffed the air and caught no sign of Hank, Junior, Granny or Dwayne. Not good.

Staying low and close to the dilapidated buildings, I made my way toward the sound of voices.

"We have what we need," Puck said. "I have no more use for the ones in chains, but I want Essie to go with us."

Awesome, that was exactly what I wanted to do with my life...be the egg slave to a smarmy Dragon. Not happening.

"Absolutely not," Tina #3 screeched. The two others voiced their displeasure quite vocally as well.

Puck Flare's roar was no small thing, and from the sound of it, the Tinas concurred. I could feel the heat and I was outside of the building. The sound of screams and slapping followed. Had he set them on fire? If they stop, drop and roll they'd live, but...

"You have almost outlived your usefulness," he hissed as the women moaned and whimpered. "What happened to Peter and Paul? You told me to plan a bogus meeting to throw the Sheriff off and now they're not here when I need them," he roared.

"They'll be here," Tina #2 assured him, sobbing.

"Peter has the formula on him and I need it now," he said coldly. "This operation will go up in flames, pun intended, if I don't have their assistance. If something has happened, I will burn this town to ashes and use you three as kindling."

"Well, that would suck the big one," Junior whispered in my ear as he slid his hand over my mouth and thankfully trapped my answering scream on its way out.

"Why can't I smell you?" I whispered as I punched him in the chest.

"Ouch." He rubbed his pecs and I rolled my eyes. "I added a new compound to the tanner. Completely erases scent. Vamps can't even detect it."

He was brilliant, but he was alone.

"Where are the others?"

"We had a little situation at the station." He grinned and chuckled. His calm amazed me.

"Spill," I said as I pulled him to a safer spot behind another broken down building.

"Your buddy Dwayne did the mind meld thing and it went a bit awry."

"Oh god, is he okay?" The thought of losing Dwayne was incomprehensible to me.

"He's fine. So are Hank and your granny," he added quickly. "But the Dragons..." He winced and gagged.

"What?"

"They're not so fine."

"Define not so fine," I said.

"They exploded." He turned a greenish hue and I backed away just in case he felt the need to hurl.

"How in the heck did they explode? Are they dead?" *Was this some kind of Dragon trick?*

"Oh, they're dead alright. Dwayne mumbled some Vampyre voodoo and the Dragons' skin started bubbling and before you could say, Dolly Parton's built like a brick shit house, they blew up like a freakin' bomb. Their guts are spread all the way from Main Street to Hangman's Trail."

That was a full six blocks. Impossible. I actually felt the need to hurl. I settled for a small gag and attempted to compartmentalize the visual. Also impossible.

"Dwayne did that?"

"Yep. Yep, he did." Junior shook his head in wonder. "No clue how we're gonna explain that one to the humans. Lots of community activities coming up; the Watermelon Festival, the Treasure Hunt, the Potato Sack Olympics…It's a damn mess and smells like hell."

"Septic," I muttered. "Tell them city septic exploded."

"Might work." He nodded. "Saw the girls. They told me what was happening. Crazy shit. I wanted them to run, but they were having none of it."

"I know." I sighed and ran my hand through my hair. "Apparently the Dragons at the meeting in town had the formula on them. I do believe what they're trying to do is a three Dragon job. If they don't come back, and clearly that's not happening, Puck will incinerate the town."

"Caught that part," Junior said as he carefully handed me a squirt gun. As I examined it, wondering if he'd lost his mind, he grabbed my wrist and immobilized me. "Shit's dangerous, Essie."

"It's a squirt gun."

"Yes, Einstein. It's a squirt gun. A squirt gun that has a liquid in it that will inhibit a shift—stop it completely. The one thing we can't let happen is to allow a Dragon to shift. None of us stands a chance against a pissed off psychotic flying reptile the size of a football stadium."

He was correct. Wolves were deadly, but Dragons beat us on size alone…not to mention the fire thing.

"Did we happen to get the formula before Dwayne blew them up?" I asked.

Junior rolled his eyes and grunted. I took that as a no. Did it matter? Dragons were notoriously selfish and greedy—at least that's what I'd always heard. There was a very good chance each of them had played a specific role and didn't show their hand even to each other. It would certainly ensure they needed each other. Or to be more precise…wouldn't kill each other. It would also explain why Puck was so furious they weren't back yet.

Holy hell, I didn't want to be around when Dragon Puck found out they'd been turned to goop.

"I need to go in there and douse the Dragon right now," I said.

"You're almost correct," Hank said from behind me. Junior slapped his hand over my mouth and stifled my screaming again for the second time in five minutes. Hank had definitely used the self tanner too. "But I'm sure you meant *we*. *We* need to go douse the Dragon and then tear him to shreds."

I glanced over at the man who made my world right and I grinned. "Yes, I'm sure I meant to say that."

"What about the she-wolves?" Junior asked.

Hank put his finger to his lips and pointed. The Tinas were making their way back to the holding room where the girls were. Their hair and clothing was singed and they appeared shell shocked and pissed. Crap.

"Junior, go around this building, come up in the rear and protect the girls. I'd like the Tinas alive, but you have my blessing to use deadly force," Hank told his brother.

"There's nothing I'd enjoy more, little bro. Where's Granny?"

"She stayed in town. Go, go, go."

Junior quickly shifted and left.

"Dwayne?" I inquired.

"He's also in town doing crowd control, seeing as he was the one who caused the massive disaster."

"You left a Vampyre and my granny in charge?" I was shocked and impressed.

"Not just any Vampyre...A three hundred year old gay drag queen Vampyre who can blow up Dragons."

Hank put his hand over his mouth, closed his eyes and gathered himself for a moment. I was becoming increasingly more relieved that I'd missed Dwayne's new party trick.

"Your buddy is apparently the hit of Hung. The crowds started chanting 'Gaga' as soon as they saw him. They were listening to him more than they were listening to me, so I told him he and Granny were running the show and to clean up his mess. Then I left."

He shrugged and grimaced.

"Plan?" I asked.

"Your call."

I swelled with pride that Hank was going to follow my lead. The simple fact that he trusted me meant the world.

"He has fertilized eggs in there somewhere. We need to get them and any computers or files we find."

"Wait. Eggs? Fertilized?"

"They're trying to crossbreed species, dismantle the Council, and take over the world."

"That was nice and succinct." His eyebrow shot up and I flipped him the bird.

"I'm good like that." I grinned and gave him a quick kiss. "I'll go in first and pretend I was running from the Tinas... I'll tell him they were trying to kill me—that I'm scared. I'll throw myself in his arms and squirt him."

Hank pressed his fingers to the bridge of his nose, a sure sign of *I don't like this plan*...I ignored his body language and went on. "As soon as he's wet, you come in and shoot him in non-kill spots. We'll restrain him and I'll find the evidence."

"Nope, not gonna work."

"Why isn't it going to work?"

"You have to get him in the eyes or mouth to make the solution work." He winced, started to say something and stopped.

"What? Spit it out. We don't have time," I said.

"I cannot believe what I'm about to say, but..."

"Say it," I hissed.

"You drank Dwayne's blood. Yes?"

"Yes."

"The solution won't harm a Vamp and even if it stops your shift, I can shift if I need to."

"What are you saying?"

"I'm saying you need to put some of the liquid in your mouth and kiss the bastard so we get it where it needs to go," he ground out unhappily. His fists were balled up and his face had flushed red with fury. "I am sick that I just suggested that."

"It's brilliant and that's exactly what I'm going to do. Yes, it's disgusting, but I really want to leave here alive today. Just stay outside until you hear me tell him, um...tell him how hot his lips are. Do you get the double entendre thingie I just said?"

He rolled his eyes and groaned.

"I thought it was pretty good," I muttered.

"Inspired," he snapped. "Put the crap in your mouth and let's do this. I'm going in human. I'm going to try not to shift unless it's necessary. Even losing a second with a Dragon is deadly. He can still blow fire in his human form. As far as guns go, their healing power is extraordinary and guns are useless. We'll have to go hand to hand and break his neck. It won't kill him, but we can restrain him. I fight first and you destroy whatever you find as far as the experiment goes. On the outside chance we die in there, I don't want him leaving with anything which can be used to make a Wolf-Dragon. If I'm losing you can jump in and help me, but it will be more of a distraction than an advantage if I'm trying to defend you."

"I find that insulting," I snapped.

"Have you ever fought a Dragon?"

"Have you?" I shot back.

He stared at me long and hard and I realized he had. He had fought a Dragon. When in the hell had Hank fought a Dragon and how did I not know this?

"Just stay away from his mouth and nose once he's pissed and we might come out of this in one piece."

"How do you know all this?" *How did he know all of this?* This was info I'd never heard.

"Because I'm..."

"Where are they?" Puck bellowed. "Everything I've worked for is going to hell. I will kill all of them."

"Go. Now."

I quickly squirted some of the liquid in my mouth as I ran toward the door of the building where Puck Flame, the assjacket, was having a hissy fit. The taste was so foul, my eyes watered. Dang it... No, that was good. Crying was good. My inner wolf jerked and fought inside of me, realizing she was trapped. I had no time to calm her. I pushed her down and burst through the door. Eyes wild and body trembling, I took in the scene.

The room was positively high tech. It had been completely refurbished—had to have taken months to create a lab this sophisticated. This was no haphazard operation. Medical tools, computers and vials littered the counters. There was a metal gurney in the center of the room with thick straps attached to it. My stomach roiled as I realized what had happened to my Pack members on that table. Monitors beeped and small petri dishes were cooking under fluorescent lights. Bingo for the eggs.

"What are you doing in here?" Puck demanded, advancing on me.

I shook my head violently and let my tears flow. Speech was impossible or I'd lose the solution.

His demeanor changed lightening fast and an unfamiliar scent filled the room. *Oh hell to the no*, he was aroused as evidenced by the bulge in his pants.

Use it. Make it work.

Moaning, I threw myself into his arms and rubbed my body against his. It was all I could do not to gag. Between the liquid in my mouth and the disgusting man running his hands over my body I was in hell.

"Are you all right, sweet thing? Did those girls try to hurt you?" he cooed and pulled me flush against his huge frame. Thank god, Hank was outside. This was nothing I wanted him to see.

I shook my head yes and wove my fingers in his hair, pulling his face toward me. He needed no more of an invitation to crush his lips to mine. He forced my mouth open and plundered inside. I spit the solution into his mouth and he jerked back as if burned.

"My god," he sputtered as his lips puckered unattractively and he coughed. "For such an exquisite girl you have appalling oral hygiene. You need to brush your teeth. Immediately."

"But your lips are so hot," I shouted and almost burst out laughing at the puzzled look of horror on his face.

Hank came through the door and everything froze for a moment. Confusion ripped across the Dragon's face quickly replaced by an anger so intense I almost turned away. How an animal with this much power and ire had been kept at bay by the Council for so many years was mind boggling.

Hank's power and magic filled the room, and the Dragon looked startled for a brief second. To be honest, I was a little thrown too. When in the hell did Hank get so deadly? The Dragon spread his arms and began to chant.

Nothing. Nothing happened.

His eyes narrowed and the chant became frantic. Hank and I stood our ground and waited. There was power in stillness. Let him play his hand first. Let his fury make him sloppy. We needed any advantage we could get.

Puck Flare's eyes turned blood red and narrowed to slits. "What have you done to me?" he demanded as a spear of fire flew from his lips. "What have you done?"

Ducking so I didn't fry was necessary, but he did ask a question. I'd been raised in the South and was occasionally polite. The man deserved an answer.

"I leveled the playing field," I told him.

"There is no playing field," he roared. "I am the superior being here. You are dirt beneath my feet."

"That's not very nice," Hank drawled. "I think you should apologize."

"You think I should *what?*"

The Dragon was icy and calm. Surely that was not a good sign. He moved toward us as smoke wafted from his nose and ears.

Everything moved in slow motion...and then it didn't.

It was violent and bloody and I was frozen in shock. The sounds of breaking bones and grunts filled the room. The two men were locked together, fighting for their lives and all I could do was watch in horror. It was almost balletic in its precision and I had no idea who was winning.

Snapping jaws with bloodstained mouths tore at each other.

Holding back was killing me, but Hank was right. He was physically stronger and it seemed like he knew what he was doing.

"Essie, destroy the eggs," Hank shouted as he took a sharp right hook to the face.

Moving with Vampyre speed, I grabbed a large, heavy tin and began smashing everything on the counters and walls. The Dragon wailed and my blood curdled. I didn't look back and I didn't stop. My job was as important as Hank's. If we died, we would not die in vain. Dying was not on my agenda, but the sound of the battle behind me was nauseating. I quickly crushed the last vials beneath my feet as the Dragon roared with such volume and ire I had to slap my hands over my ears to keep my eardrums from bursting.

Done. I was done. Nothing in the room was salvageable. Wait a minute. I had moved with Vamp speed...I had Vamp strength. What was I thinking?

Turning back to the fight, I tried to find an opening. The Dragon had the Wolf by the neck. Hank struggled and elbowed the Dragon with such force that he flew backward. Both men were in bad shape. Watching time was over. It was my turn to play.

"Hey Puck, I ate a mint. Do you wanna make out now?" The utter ridiculousness of my statement threw him off his game long enough for Hank to pin him. I dove forward and narrowly avoided the explosion of flames Puck aimed at me. Reaching for his neck while Hank had him down was my goal. The vicious head butt to my face was unexpected and my eye began to swell shut immediately.

"Hey...asswipe. That hurt," I shouted as I pummeled his face, landing a jarring left hook to his nose. The crunch of bone under my fist was sickening, but I wanted more. I was so intent on getting to his neck I completely missed the fact that I was fighting him alone. Hank was on fire and rolling on the floor to put himself out.

"You think that hurt, you little bitch?" the Dragon hissed viciously. "I will make you hurt so badly you will beg for death."

I saw the fist coming before it landed and he was right. Several more of those and I *would* beg for death. New goal...avoid the fist. Jumping back, I dropped into a fighting stance and waited for his next move. He laughed and winked.

"I like your spirit — you would have been a good egg donor. Too bad you have to die."

He lunged and I moved to my left, raising my knee and propelling it into his Adam's apple as he went for me.

The sheer force I had used surprised me. Again, I mentally kissed Dwayne. However, my strength surprised the Dragon even more. Defensive fighting was no longer an option. I fought with everything I had, but so did he.

The sound of bones snapping was sickening, especially because they were mine, but I healed instantly. Using a combination of martial arts and sheer brute force I was holding my own...*barely*. Blood ran from my forehead, my nose and god knew where else. I wasn't going to last much longer. At least I'd destroyed his masterpiece...

The howl from my mate chilled me to the bone. Hank was dying and the Dragon had killed him. I had nothing left to lose. Nothing. The Dragon made the mistake of glancing in the direction of the sound and I knew I had one last opening. Without thinking, I sprang forward, grabbed his head and twisted for all I was worth. The shrill scream and the bones unhinging under my fingers gave me power I didn't know I possessed. I had no idea if Hank was alive or dead, but I was going out fighting. I twisted and I twisted. I yanked, grunted and howled.

Hot liquid covered my hands and made my grip slippery, but I held on. No letting go. If I let go, I die. Break his neck, restrain him. Break it and we might live. Break. Snap. Destroy. Hurt the Dragon like he had hurt my friends—like he had hurt the Panther and Bear Shifters that had died because he wanted to play God.

Dwayne's Vampyre blood running through my veins stung. The fury and desperation I felt was my own, but it was mixed with something unfamiliar and terrifying. I needed to get to Hank and make him shift...give him my blood, make him drink. But if I let go, I would be lost. Twist. Twist.

He hadn't even asked me to marry him yet. He couldn't die before he asked me to marry him. Twist and pull.

Dwayne was going to wear a dress and Granny was going to give me away.

Break the neck. My weeping sounded distant to my own ears.

Gushing blood and tears blurred my vision. Twist...break.

"Essie, stop." Hanks voice was harsh, but he didn't understand. The Dragon was going to kill us. I just needed to twist one more time.

"Look at me," Hank demanded. "Now."

I stopped and stared. He was alive and I was too. Had I broken the Dragon's neck? Was he restrained? I glanced down at my hands and screamed. In a death grip I held the head of a Dragon. His body lay on the other side of the room. Dead eyes stared at me and I dropped the head in horror.

"How did I do that?" I gasped and my body shook like a leaf. "I didn't know I did that. How did I not know?"

"Essie, it's okay. You're okay. The Vampyre took over and you decapitated the Dragon."

"Decapitation means to cut a head off. I yanked it off of his body," I said in a shrill voice I didn't recognize. Curling into a ball, I rocked back and forth and tried to get a handle on myself. "I don't want to be a Vampyre. It's dark and wrong."

"You're not a Vampyre. You're a wolf. Dwayne gave you—gave us—a gift. We're alive because of what you did."

"I tore his head off," I said flatly and then started to laugh. I knew I was probably in shock, but all of a sudden I was crazy happy about the fact I'd just torn the head off of a Dragon. This wasn't much different than other jobs I'd been on...*actually it was.* I'd used weapons and I'd been detached from the situation. I didn't know the victims personally and I hadn't torn their heads off with my bare hands. No amount of psychotherapy—or even a lobotomy—was going to dull the memory of this one.

"Would it have made a difference if you'd used a sword?" he asked as he gathered me in his arms.

"I don't know. I'm bleeding on you," I muttered.

"Yes, and I'm bleeding on you. You saved our lives. I was on fire, for god's sake. We should be dead." He held me close and his body shuddered. "You do realize we'll have to name our first child Dwayne."

That gave me pause. As much as I loved Dwayne, I wasn't crazy about his name. "Do we have to?" I asked.

"Yep." Hank grinned and pulled me to my feet. "Come on, Essie the Ripper. We need to check on the others."

"I think I would have felt bad even if I'd used a sword."

"Why? You did what you had to do."

"Honestly, I don't feel bad about killing him. It was him or us. I feel bad about my loss of control, and the small but significant fact, that I had no clue I'd torn his noggin off of his body."

"I can see how it might seem a little odd," Hank agreed. "But it was sort of hot in a female Rambo kind of way."

"Oh, hell no. You did not get turned on by watching me rip a dude's head from his shoulders?"

"No. That part was actually fairly gross. It was watching you fight and own it. You were a machine." He held me tight to his body and I drank in his strength and calm.

"You know, this Vampyre thing will wear off and I won't be such a machine anymore," I said as I snuggled closer.

"I'm good with that." He laughed and pulled me from the carnage. "I'll take you any way I can get you."

"Ditto," I said and never looked back once. "And if you ever call me Essie the Ripper again, I'll rip something off you to prove I'm a woman of my word."

"Duly noted."

Chapter 14

The Tinas were bound in silver chains and hung upside down. Appropriately, the evil she-wolves hung from the very same rusted out pipes the girls had been attached to. They were missing teeth, and from the smell, they'd clearly had a little upchuck session. Junior was in the corner staring at Sandy Moongie like a love struck puppy. Hmmmmm.

"You look like hell," Sandy said as she looked me up and down, not looking much better herself. "I sure hope the other guy looks worse."

"He does."

"Is he dead?" Junior asked.

"Quite," Hank told him.

I was relieved Hank didn't go into details. I wasn't sure it was a story I wanted told. Ever.

"We didn't kill them," Debbie said, referring to the strangely subdued Tinas. "We would be no better than them if we did."

"But we fought, Essie. We defended ourselves like you said." Frankie grinned bashfully and wiped the blood from an ugly gash she sported.

"They were something to be reckoned with," Junior said with pride, eyes still glued to Sandy. "These gals had it covered. I just stood back and watched."

I caught a quick exchange of sexually charged glances between Sandy and Junior and I bit back a grin.

"I have their teeth if you want them." Jenny tried to hand me a collection of bloodstained pearly whites.

"Um, no. While I'm honored and proud of you and um...no."

Jenny grinned and shoved the teeth in her pocket as the gals fist bumped each other in victory. As we contemplated what to do with the traitors, a shrill hiss and a gust of icy wind ripped through the room. Everyone gasped in terror and ducked for cover. *Could a Dragon live with no head?*

"I was amazing," Dwayne squealed triumphantly as he landed gracefully in the middle of the room. "I did the meld and they bubbled and turned a lovely bluish-orange-green and then BOOM! The sound was incredible. Absolutely fabulous—like fornicating cats and Madonna."

"Holy hell, did you fly here?" I asked as I got shakily back to my feet and decided not to broach the cat/Madonna thing.

"You had the car keys. What was I supposed to do? This place is a disaster. Of course, it's not quite as bad as downtown," Dwayne announced as he took in the room.

"Understatement," Hank muttered and Dwayne grinned evilly.

"It is a mess," Junior agreed. "Who's gonna clean this up?"

"The Council is cleaning up the debacle," Dwayne informed us victoriously. "I called up your boss, Angela, and read her the riot act. I got her up to speed and then I tore her a new one. I forbid her to send you into anything so dangerous again. I have been worried sick and that is not good for my digestion. I told her to send down a crew because there are Dragon innards covering half the town and I assumed there would be more to take care of out here. Do you want me to mind meld the Tinas?" He cocked his head toward the hanging traitors.

"No!" everyone yelled in unison.

"Just a suggestion," Dwayne huffed, completely offended.

"Well, I don't know about you, but I want to get out of here," Frankie said.

"What time is it?" Dwayne asked frantically. "I have a show tonight and I'm doing all three *Charlie's Angels*."

The girls looked confused. "Don't ask," I said. "Let it be a surprise."

"Do we just leave them?" Sandy asked.

"For the moment, yes," Hank said as the Tinas hissed and swore. "Enough," he bellowed.

The Tinas whimpered and everyone else flinched. I might be the alpha's mate, but Hank was definitely the alpha.

"You have disgraced yourselves and this Pack," he went on coldly. "Your behavior merits death, but that is far too good for you. You will be shunned. I will leave you in your final hours of belonging to a Pack and let you think about what you have done. After tomorrow I never want to lay eyes on you again."

We filed out and left the Tinas hanging upside down in the holding cell. We heard their sobs as we formed a circle outside.

"We'll shift and run back. It's the fastest way and everyone needs to heal," Hank instructed. "I want everyone at the sheriff's office. We'll notify your families and tonight we celebrate."

No one cheered. We were too tired and still in shock, but heartfelt smiles were shared.

"Essie, can I ride you back to town?" Dwayne asked.

"No, you can't."

"Fine. It can't hurt to ask." He grinned and levitated into the air.

Everyone shifted except Hank and me. We watched as our Pack made their way home. The beauty of the wolves always left me breathless. Knowing I was also one of the magical creatures awed me.

"Can you shift yet?" Hank asked.

"I don't know," I admitted. My wolf felt lethargic inside me, but she was pleased. "You do realize you have some explaining to do, Mr. Dragon Slayer."

"I didn't slay the Dragon, pretty girl. You did."

"You know what I mean."

He stared at me for a long minute with a sexy half grin on his face. "It might piss you off."

"It would take a whole hell of a lot to piss me off at the moment, so unless you're married with ten kids, in which case I'd kill you...now might be a good time to confess," I told him as my body tensed.

What in the world could he tell me? He was half Dragon? Impossible. His new hobby was offing Dragons? Unlikely. I waited impatiently.

"I'm WTF."

Not what I expected. *At all.* "Right." I laughed and waited for the punch line. It didn't come. "What do you mean you're WTF?"

"When I discovered where you were and what you were doing I watched you."

"You mean stalked me?"

"Some might define it as stalking." He grinned. "You were beautiful, amazing, confident and strong. I didn't think you were ever coming back to me, so I joined."

I was speechless. He was going to give up everything he loved for me?

"Why?" I whispered. "You're the alpha. You have a Pack and a career and a life..."

"Because none of it means anything without you."

My knees buckled and I crumpled to the ground. How could I ever have been so stupid to have left this man? No one in my long life would ever love me like he did. No one.

"The Pack. What about the Pack, Hank?"

"The Pack was never supposed to be mine in the first place. It just so happens my amazing mother gave birth to two alphas. I was more prepared than Junior was to take over at the time of my father's retirement."

"Junior?"

"Yep." He grinned and shook his head. "It's time for my big brother to step up and lead our Pack. He's been ready for a while, but he would have never challenged me for the position. We're far more than just two alphas—we're brothers."

"So, we're not staying in Hung?" I asked, unsure what I really wanted.

"Right now I want to leave that decision up to you. But I think Junior will have an easier transition to Pack leader if I go away for at least a little while."

I mulled over everything I had just learned and realized I felt lighter than I had in years. Could I really love the man of my dreams and still do what I'd become passionate about? Stuff like this never happened for me...

"Hank, my parents..." I couldn't get it out. It hurt. Why after so long did their death cause physical pain? *Maybe because they didn't have to die.*

"I already know," he said as he wrapped me in his arms. "Granny told me."

She'd certainly been busy, but I was grateful I didn't have to speak the horrible story out loud. My Granny loved me fierce, even if she couldn't keep her damned mouth shut.

"We'll go," I said firmly. "We'll go back to Chicago and let Junior find his place. I have to find out what happened to my parents and..."

"We. We have to find out what happened to your parents and then we will figure out what's next."

I laid my head on his chest and listened to his heartbeat—so strong, sure and mine. No matter what else life handed me, I knew my first priority would be to take care of the alpha who loved me.

"I feel very attached to you right now," I whispered as I breathed in his scent.

"I can work with that." He chuckled and held me tighter.

"I'm also feeling the need to jump your bones."

"As much as it pains me to take a rain check, and let me be very clear...it pains me," he said, referring to the impressive bulge in his jeans. "But I think we should get back to town and make sure our people are okay."

Reluctantly, I slid from his arms and stood up. "I agree, but I will take a rain check."

"That's good because it's definitely going to rain tonight. All night."

"You sure about that, Big Boy?" I giggled.

"Never been more sure about anything in my life. Can you shift?" he asked as he gently tucked my wildly messy hair behind my ear.

I closed my eyes and drew on the power of my inner wolf. She was there and she was ready. "Yes. I can."

We quickly removed our torn and bloody clothing as the magic engulfed us. A magic so wondrous and rare it always humbled me. My skin changed to fur, my bones shifted painlessly, and my body became what it was meant to be. My wolf—my strong and beautiful wolf.

Hank's wolf was breath taking. His shiny chocolate coat glistened in the sun. He was much larger than me in his Lycan form, but his eyes were the same mesmerizing green. He nipped at my nose as I mooned at his beauty.

"*You gonna just stare at me or are you gonna to race me back to town?*" His amused voiced bounced through my head and I giggled.

"*I'm gonna kick your Wolfy ass,*" I challenged as I took off leaving him in the dust.

The wind in my fur and the sun beginning to dip on the horizon into the ocean made this day one I would not soon forget. Of course, ripping the head off of a Dragon did figure in, but running with wild abandon next to my mate made me complete. No matter where we went, Hank would always be my home. That's the part that would stay with me. Always.

Epilogue

The shunning of the traitors was anticlimactic compared to everything else that had happened. The vote among the Pack was unanimous. The findings were reported to the Council and approved without contest. The Tinas were gone and would not be missed. No Pack anywhere in the world would accept them. I tried to find it within myself to feel pity, but I couldn't. Perhaps with time I might, but it was still too raw.

The families of the missing girls were ecstatic to have them home. Hank, Junior and I were the local heroes, but Dwayne...Dwayne was the Second Coming.

All the Weres in our community bowed their heads in reverence when he passed. Even the more conservative Weres caught all of his shows at the drag club. The owner had to make a special dispensation for children because the Weres had insisted the young ones witness the talent of their savior.

Dwayne was in absolute heaven.

The Council had quietly sent down a crew to clean up Hung and the deserted resort on the outskirts of town. No one even knew they were here. Apparently they had come in the middle of the night and were gone by morning. My guess was they had sent Hyenas. Those shifters would eat anything—including Dragon guts. I tried not to dwell on it because thinking about it made me a little nauseous.

To make reparations for their misguided judgment—*their words, definitely not mine*—the Council purchased the old resort from the city and planned to restore it to a haven which would make people forget about its tragic history. All the proceeds would go to the Pack. It was yet again the Council putting a tiny Band-Aid on a gaping wound, but my fight with the Council would come in good time.

My boss, Angela was a different story. Her visit to Hung Island, Georgia was quick and to the point.

"Those bastard Dragons are being investigated much to their displeasure," Angela grunted as she sat on the plastic slip covered couch in my granny's house. My boss had brought her own bottle of whiskey and was indulging liberally. She was sporting a new and rather large bald spot over her left ear. She really needed to consider a new vocation.

"Yeah, well they should be," I said as I dug into a Juju's Meat-Lovers Pizza. "What they did was horrific and I'd bet Dwayne's Laboutin pumps that more were involved."

"My thoughts exactly," she agreed. "Those fire blowers need to be doused."

Hank, Granny and Dwayne had joined the impromptu pizza party. Hank was quiet, Granny was downright mute, but Dwayne was as animated as ever. My boss was formally polite. However, I was waiting for the other shoe to drop...it always did.

"She banged him," Dwayne happily informed Angela. "You owe me money."

"Actually you owe me money," she shot back.

"How do you figure that?" Dwayne asked, confused.

"You bet five hundred she would bang him and I bet a thousand you were right. You owe me five hundred."

"Damn it to hell," Dwayne muttered as he pulled out his wallet and removed five crisp one hundred dollar bills. "I need to listen a little better when I gamble."

"So, little missy, what are your plans?" Angela's eyes narrowed at me, but her voice wavered slightly.

I was different now. I knew it and she knew it. No longer was I the scattered dingbat I had been only weeks ago. Well that might be pushing it, but I *had* ripped the head off a Dragon. If that didn't change a gal, I didn't know what would.

I grinned and gave her a non-committal shrug that made her reach into her hair and pull hard.

"And you—Mr. Special-Forces-I-Exist-in-No-Data-Base—what are your plans?" she asked Hank getting more nervous with each non answer. "Are you coming back to Chicago?"

"That depends on a few things," Hank said as he leaned back in his chair and crossed his legs casually. Nothing Hank did was casual. Nothing.

"What things?" Angela asked. I felt kind of sorry for her. I liked her, but she no longer had my trust. I wondered how deeply she was involved with the Council and how much she really knew about my past and my parents.

"Essie goes off the radar too," he said calmly as if he was discussing the weather, but his deadly magic drenched the room. Angela shifted uncomfortably and Dwayne clapped his hands with glee. "We'll take missions, but we will answer to no one. We will report to you and you can keep the Council aware of our movements."

Angela's silence and terse nod shocked me, but Hank's demands shocked me even more. He was way more than an agent like me. He had some major explaining to do, but now was not the time.

"After Essie completes the next mission, she has a free pass to get out," Granny hissed from the corner of the room where she sat with her hands fisted in her lap.

"I wondered when you'd talk, Bobbie Sue," Angela said quietly making it very clear to me that the women knew each other. "That's not my call, but I will see what I can do. Are you in?"

Granny stared Angela down until she squirmed and tugged on her quickly disappearing hair. Then my granny shrugged. "I've been out for forty years, but as much as I don't like you, I like the Dragons even less. I'm in."

"Color me confused and clueless, but what in the hell is going on here?" I demanded.

Granny ignored me and continued to pin Angela with a stare that made me want to pee in my pants. "Dwayne is my second. We also go off the radar and Essie is out when we're done. No negotiations."

The silence in the room was deafening and the story was one I would pull out of my granny even if she tried to whoop my ass in the process. As much as I wanted answers, I knew when to keep my mouth shut.

"Deal." Angela sighed and dropped her head to her hands in defeat. "Be in Chicago on Monday and I will..."

"No can do," Dwayne said. The silly Vampyre was gone and in his place was a very powerful supernatural bald freak of nature. "We have a vacation planned and I am not going to postpone it. This mission, *as you call it*, has dead Werewolf and Vampyre written all over it. Before I turn to dust, I am going to drink blood-laced alcoholic beverages with pineapple and pink-jeweled umbrellas in them. Essie and Hank are newly mated and have some urgent business to attend to or else they will be useless walking hormones. Granny needs to experience a nude beach and I need to find a sexy Rastafarian wig for my Bob Marley impersonation. Plus, I bought eight new Speedos and I plan to get good use out of them."

"You're doing men in the drag show now?" I asked, surprised. Not the most appropriate question at the moment, considering the tension in the room, but I just had to know.

"Only Bob Marley and David Hasselhoff," Dwayne squealed and then morphed right back into scary Vampyre dude. "We'll report to Chicago in two weeks. Period."

"Fine," Angela capitulated wearily. "Where are you going?"

"Jamaica." Dwayne grinned from ear to ear. "We're going to Jamaica."

***

"Oh my god almighty and Cher pre-surgery, I could live here the rest of my days and be happy," Dwayne gushed as we watched the ocean waves crash against the rocks. "If I had hair I'd get it braided and skip along the beach while it whipped me in the eyes."

I rolled my eyes. Thankfully, he was bald.

"Jamaica is nice," Granny mused. "But I miss the rednecks."

She adjusted her thong bikini and I closed my eyes in agony. There was only so much I wanted to see of my granny and her naked butt wasn't one of them. We'd all decided to postpone the necessary talks about Granny's past and Hank's nefarious skills until our vacation was over. I was more than okay with that. If we were all going to bite it soon, I wanted to have a week of fun in the sun.

"Where's Hank?" I asked with my eyes still squeezed shut.

No one answered.

"I said, where's Ha…"

I opened my eyes slowly, prepared to glue them shut if Granny had decided to go topless. My tummy dropped and my heart raced. Granny and Dwayne stood quietly by the shore with their backs to me. Hank was in front of me on one knee. In lieu of screaming or passing out, I dropped to my knees and held on to him for dear life.

"I'm pretty sure only one of us is supposed to be on their knees." His lopsided grin made me weak and I giggled like an idiot.

"My legs quit working," I stammered. "And I thought I might make you more comfortable…then a heavy metal band started a concert in my stomach and then my legs turned to jelly, and then I, um…"

"You done?"

"It would probably be a good thing if I was."

"Probably." He laughed and I felt heat crawl up my neck and land on my face.

He put his hand under my chin and raised my eyes to his. "Ester Elizabeth McGee, I have loved you since the moment I saw you many years ago. You are the other half to my whole. I promise to love you always and never let you go. You make me better and stronger and my life means nothing when you're not in it." He took a deep breath and his eyes glistened silver in the Jamaican sun. "Essie, I love you. Will you marry me?"

The screaming took me by surprise. Who in the hell was making that racket? I glanced down to the water's edge at Granny and Dwayne. They were not screaming. Hank was not screaming. There was no one else on the beach.

It was me. I was screaming and crying and blubbering. Hank's laugh made me want to slug him, but I wanted to kiss him more.

"Does that mean yes?" he asked as he trapped me in a hug so tight I could barely breathe, but I didn't care. It felt so very right—so very perfect.

I nodded my head because I was terrified I would start screaming again.

"She said yes," he yelled as Granny and Dwayne tore over to us.

"Where's the ring?" Dwayne demanded, possibly more excited than me.

Hank pulled a beautiful diamond ring with a cushion cut stone from a pocket in his shorts, slid it on my finger and I gasped. It was redonkulously large and real and I loved it, but I loved him even more. I slapped my hand over my mouth to stem the babbling dialogue that threatened to fly out. Tears clouded my vision and my breath came in short gasps.

In my many imaginings of this moment, I had handled it with sexy grace. Real life had turned out vastly different than I expected, but it was no less wonderful. My joy matched my mate's and my need to throw him to the ground and tackle him was overwhelming...so I did.

Granny and Dwayne slipped away and disappeared as I rolled down the beach tangled up in the most beautiful man in the world. The only thing stopping me from doing something illegal was the sheer amount of sand that had gathered in my bikini bottoms.

"I will marry you, Henry James Wilson. I will love you always. Next time I have a stupid idea, I promise I will run it past you first."

Hank held me close and pressed sweet kisses all over my face. "That works for me, Essie. You're mine."

"And you're mine."

He laughed and picked me up in his strong arms. "Yes, I'm yours. Now I'd really like to shower the sand out of my pants. You with me?"

"I am with you till the end of time. I do have some sand in some unmentionable places," I mumbled. "Maybe you could help me out with that?"

"I think it could be arranged. I definitely think it could be arranged."

And it was. And it was amazing. Really, really amazing...really, really.

THE END (for now)

NOTE FROM THE AUTHOR: If you enjoyed this book, please consider leaving a positive review or rating on the site where you purchased it. Reader reviews help my books continue to be valued by distributors/resellers and help new readers make decisions about reading them. You are the reason I write these stories and I sincerely appreciate you!

Many thanks for your support,
~ Robyn Peterman

Visit me on my website at
http://www.robynpeterman.com.

In the back of this book, you will find extended excerpts from two of my paranormal series. I hope you enjoy these samples. The stories are available in both ebook and print at your favorite retailers. Links to them are also located on my website.

Excerpt from

Switching Hour

Chapter One

"If you say or do anything that sends our asses back to the magic pokey, I will zap you bald and give you a cold sore that makes you look like you were born with three lips."

I tried to snatch the scissors from my best friend's hand, but I might as well have been trying to catch a greased cat.

"Look at my hair," she hissed, holding up her bangs. "They're touching my nose—my fucking *nose,* Zelda. I can't be seen like this when we get out. I swear I'll just do it a little."

"Winnifred, you have never done anything just a little. What happened the last time you cut your own bangs?"

She winced and mumbled her shame into her collarbone. "That was years ago. They rebuilt the building and no one was killed."

"Fine," I snapped. "Cut your bangs, but don't come crying to me when you look like the dude from *Dumb and Dumber.*"

"You know what?" she shouted, brandishing the shears entirely too close to my head for comfort, "we're here because of you, asshead."

That stopped me dead in my pursuit of saving her from herself. What the hell did I care? Let her cut her bangs up to her hairline and suffer the humiliation of looking five. Maybe I wasn't completely innocent here, but I bore far less of the blame than she did.

"No. We're in here because of you, Winnifred."

She rolled her eyes. "No. It was definitely you, Zelda."

"You."

"Nope—*you.*"

Winnie's selective memory was messing with my need to protect my ass. "Oh my Goddess," I yelled. "I didn't sleep with Baba Yaga's precious nephew—you did."

Winnie blinked in faux innocence, her long dark lashes sweeping her cheek. "First of all, we didn't sleep. And how in the hell was I supposed to know Mr. Sexy Pants was her nephew?"

"Um, well, let me see…did the fact that his name was *Benny Yaga* not ring any fucking bells?"

I was so done. It was *not* my fault we were in here and it was time Winnie accepted her responsibility in the matter.

"Well, it's not like the Council put you in here just to keep me company. You ran over your own familiar. *On purpose*," she accused.

I watched in horror as she combed her bangs forward in preparation for blast off and willed myself not to give a rat's ass.

"I did not run over that mangy bastard cat on purpose. The little shit stepped under my wheel."

"Three times?" she inquired politely.

"Yes."

We glared at each other until we were both biting back grins so hard it hurt. I couldn't stay mad at her and she couldn't stay mad at me. We'd known and loved each other far too long to stay angry. Plus, I was grateful for her presence. It would have sucked to serve time alone.

"I really need a mirror to do this right," Winnie muttered. She mimed the cutting action by lining up her fingers up on her hair before she commenced.

Our cell was barren of all modern conveniences, especially those we could perform magic with, like mirrors. We were locked up in Salem, Massachusetts in a hotel from the 1900s that had been converted to a jail for witches. Our home away from home was cell block D, designated for witches who abused their magic as easily as they changed their underwear.

From the outside the decrepit building was glamoured to look like a charming bed and breakfast complete with climbing ivy and flowers growing out of every conceivable nook and cranny. Inside it was cold and ugly with barren brick walls covered with Goddess knew what kind of slime. It was warded heavily with magic, keeping all mortals and responsible magic-makers away. At the moment Winnie and I were the only two inhabitants in the charming hell-hole. Well, us and the humor-free staff of older than dirt witches and warlocks.

I dropped onto my cot and ran my hands through my mass of uncontrollable auburn curls which looked horrid with the orange prison wear. The first thing I was going to do when I got out was burn the jumpsuit and buy out Neiman's.

"Fine. We're both here because we messed up, but I still think nine months was harsh for killing a revolting cat and screwing an idiot."

Winnie's gaze became distant and thoughtful, the way it always did when that night with Benny Yaga was mentioned. "He wasn't an idiot, but I agree. We're both guilty," she replied as she went for the first snip.

I held my breath and then blew it out as Winnie put the scissors down and changed her mind.

"I can't do this right now. I really need a mirror."

"In an hour you'll have one unless we do something stupid," I told her and then froze.

Without warning the magic level in the B&B changed drastically—the stench of centuries-old voodoo drifted to my nose. Winnie latched onto me for purchase, her eyes wide.

"Do you smell it?" I whispered. I knew her grip would leave marks, but right now that was the least of our problems.

"I do," she murmured back.

"Old lady crouch."

"What?" Her eyes grew wide and she bit down on her lip. Hard. "If you make me laugh, I'll smite your sorry ass when we get out. What the hell is old lady crouch?"

My grin threatened to split my face. My fear of incarceration was clearly outweighed by my need to make Winnie laugh again. "You know—the smell when you go to the bathroom at the country club...powdery old lady crouch."

"Oh my hell, Zelda." She giggled and punched me. "I won't be able to let that one go."

"Only a lobotomy can erase that one." I was proud of myself. Usually she got me, but I knew I scored with the crouch.

"Well, well, well," a nasally voice cooed from beyond the bars of our cell. "If it isn't the problem children."

Baba Yaga had to be at least three hundred if she was a day, but witches aged slowly—so she really only looked thirty-fiveish. The more powerful the witch, the slower said witch aged. Baba was powerful, beautiful and had appalling taste in clothes. Dressed right out of the movie *Flash Dance* complete with the ripped sweatshirt, leggings and headband. It was all I could do not to alert the fashion police.

She was surrounded by the rest of her spooky posse, an angry bunch of warlocks who were clearly unhappy to be in attendance.

"Baba Yaga," Winnie said respectfully.

"Your Crouchness," I muttered and received a quick elbow to the gut from Winnie.

Baba Yaga leaned against the cell bars, and her torn at the shoulder sweatshirt dripped over her creamy shoulder. "Zelda and Winnifred, you have served your term. Upon release you will have limited magic."

I gasped and Winnie paled. WTF? We'd done our time. *Limited magic?* What did that mean?

"Fuck," I stuttered.

"But...um...Ms. Yaga, that's not fair," Winnie added more eloquently than I had. "We paid our dues. We gave Chi-Chi all of our Kotex pads. Isn't that selfless enough?"

"Enough," Baba Yaga hissed as she waved a freshly painted nail at us in admonishment. "You two are on probation, and during that probation, you will be strictly forbidden to see each other until you have completed your tasks."

"*Tasks?*" Winnie muttered.

Baba Yaga nodded impatiently. "Tasks. *Selfless* tasks. And before you two get all uppity with that *'I can't believe you're being so harsh'* drivel, keep in mind that this is a light sentence. Most of the Council wanted you imbeciles stripped of your magic permanently."

That was news. What on earth had we done that would merit that? We conjured up fun things. Sure, they were things we used to our advantage, like shoes and sunny vacations with fruity drinks, sporting festive umbrellas in them, served to us on a tropical beach by guys with fine asses...but it wasn't like we took anything from anyone in the process.

"I'm not real clear here," I said warily.

"Oh, I can help with that," Baba Yaga offered kindly. "You, Zelda—how many pairs of Jimmy Choo shoes do you own?"

I mentally counted in my head—kind of. "Um...three?"

Baba Yaga frowned and bright green sparks flew around her head. "Seventy-five and you paid for none of them. Not to mention your wardrobe and cars and the embarrassingly expensive vacations you have taken for free." Her eyes narrowed dangerously and I swallowed my retort. Plus, I had eighty pairs...

"And you, Winnifred, you've used your magic to seduce men and have incurred millions in damages from your temper tantrums. Six buildings in the last eight months. Can you not see how I had to fight for you?" she demanded, her beautiful eyes fiery.

"Well, when you put it that way..." I mumbled.

"There is no other way to put it," she snapped as her mystical lynch mob nodded like the bobble-headed dorks that they were. "Zelda, you have used your magic for self-serving purposes and Winnifred, you have a temper that when combined with your magic could be deadly. We are White Witches. We use magic to heal and to make Mother Earth a better place. Not to walk the runway and take down cities."

"So what do we have to do?" Winnie asked with a tremor in her voice. She was freaked.

Baba Yaga winked and my stomach dropped to my toes. "There are two envelopes with your tasks in them. You will not share the contents with each other. If you do, you will render yourselves powerless. *Forever.* You have till midnight on All Hallows Eve to complete your assignments and then you will come under review with the Council."

"And if we are unable to fulfill our duty?" I asked, wanting to get all the facts upfront.

"You will become mortal."

Shit. On that alarming and potentially life ending note, Baba Yaga and her entourage disappeared in a cloud of old lady crouch smoke.

"Well, that's fucking craptastic," Winnie said as she warily sniffed her envelope—one that had appeared out of thin air and landed right between her fingertips.

"You took the words out of my mouth," I replied as I examined my envelope.

Winnie set hers on her cot as though she were afraid to touch it and turned her back on it. I simply shoved mine in the pocket of my heinous orange jumpsuit.

"So that's it? We just do whatever the contents of the envelope tell us to do, but we can't do it together? Okay, so we're a little self-absorbed, but I do use my magic to heal and so do you. Remember when you got the paper cut at Office Max? I totally healed it because you were bleeding all over my cute sundress."

"And then I zapped your sundress clean," I added, not to be outdone by our list of somewhat dubious selfless acts. "However, I get the feeling that's not the kind of healing magic Baba Yasshole means." I sat down on my own cot, still stunned by our sentence from the Council.

"You know what? Screw Baba Ganoush!" Winnie yelped as she grabbed her envelope and waved it in the air. I sighed and put my hand on her arm to prevent her from doing any damage to her task. "Yomamma. It's Baba Yomamma, Winnie. And seriously—what choice do we have at this point, but to do what she says? You don't want to stay in here, do you? We only have so many Kotex pads between us. I say we yank up our big girl panties and get this shit done. Deal?" I stunned myself and Winnie with my responsible reasoning ability.

Winnie made a face but nodded. "Baba Wha-Wha said we couldn't share the contents of our envelopes. There's no way in hell we can open these together and not share."

"Correct. Baba Yosuckmybutt is hateful. She knows we share everything."

"You want to share getting turned into mortals?"

I shuddered. "Fuck no. So now what?" I asked as I played with the offending envelope in my pocket.

"See you on the flip side?" Winnie held up her fist for a bump.

I bumped. "Wouldn't miss it."

Winnie grinned and I answered with my own. Adventures were never as fun without her, but the thought of becoming human was unacceptable.

"So we walk out of here on three?" she said.

"Yes, we do."

We both took a deep breath. "One, two, three..."

The door of our cell popped open the moment we approached it, clanging and creaking. We exchanged one last smile before Winnie hung a left and headed down the winding cement path that led to freedom. She made her way down the dimly lit hallway until she was nothing but a small, curvy dot on the horizon.

Something in my gut told me I wasn't going to see Winnie again like we planned and maybe I shouldn't have been so flip about saying goodbye. The idea of losing my magic was beyond unacceptable and I was sure Winnie felt the same. Baba Yobutthole meant business this time and it might just be enough to scare me straight. I couldn't lose my magic. I absolutely couldn't. Even if keeping it cost me having my best friend around. Goddess forgive me if that was the most cold and selfish I'd ever been, but I'd already lost most of the people in my life. I was used to it.

I clutched the envelope in my pocket with determination and sucked in a huge breath.

And then I hung a right.

Chapter Two

Dearest Zelda,

Apparently your Aunt Hildy died. Violently. You have inherited her home. Go there and make me proud that I didn't strip you of your magic. You will know what to do when you get there.

If you ever use the term "old lady crouch" again while referring to me I will remove your tongue.

xoxo Baba Yaga

P.S. The address is on the back of the note and there is a car for you parked in the garage under the hotel. It's the green one. The purple one is mine. If you even look at it, I will put all of your shoes up for sale on eBay. And yes, I am well aware you have eighty pairs.

"Motherhumper, what a bee-otch—put my shoes up for sale, my ass. And who in the hell is Aunt Hildy? I don't have a freakin' aunt named Hildy. Died violently? What exactly does 'died violently' mean?" I muttered to no one as I reread the ridiculous note. Goddess, I wondered what Winnie's note said, but we had gone our separate ways about an hour ago.

My mother was an only child and I hadn't seen her in years—so no Aunt Hildy on that side. My mom, *and I use the term loosely*, was an insanely powerful witch who had met some uber-hot, super weird Vampire ten years ago and they'd gone off to live in a remote castle in Transylvania. The end.

And my father...his identity was anyone's guess. In her day my mother had been a very popular and *active* witch. I suppose Baba *I Know Freakin' Everything* Yaga knew who my elusive daddy was and Hildy must be his sister. Awesome.

I hustled my ass to the garage and gasped in dismay. In the far corner of the dank, dark, musty smelling garage sat a car...a green car. A lime green car. Even better, it was a lime green Kia. Was Baba YoMamma fucking joking?

Why did I have to drive anywhere? I was a witch. I could use magic to get wherever I wanted to go.

Crap.

Did I even have enough magic to transport? Could I end up wedged in a time warp and stuck for eternity?

And what, pray tell, was this? A Porsche? Baba Yoyeastinfection drove a Porsche...of course she did.

I eyed the purple Porsche with envy and for a brief moment considered keying it. The look on Boobie Yoogie's face would be worth it, but another couple of years in the magic pokey plus having to watch my fancy footwear be auctioned off on eBay was enough to curb my impulse. However, I did lick my finger and smear it on the driver's side mirror. I was told not to look at it. The cryptic note mentioned nothing about touching it.

Glancing down at my orange jumpsuit I cringed. Did they really expect me to wear this? What the hell had become of me? I was a thirty-year-old paroled witch in orange prison wear and tennis shoes. My fingers ached to clothe myself in something cute and sassy. Did I dare? How would they even know?

Wait...she knew I called her old lady crouch. She would certainly know if I magicked up some designer duds. Shitballs. Orange outfit and red hair it was.

Thankfully the car had a GPS, not that I knew how to work anything electronic. I was a witch, for god's sake. I normally flicked my fingers or wiggled my nose. The address of my inheritance was in West Virginia. How freakin' far was West Virginia from Salem, Massachusetts?

Apparently eleven hours and twenty-one minutes.

It took me exactly forty-five minutes of swearing and punching the dashboard to figure that little nugget out. Bitchy Yicky was officially my least favorite person in the world. However, I was a little proud that I made the damn GPS work without using magic or blowing it up.

***

Five hours into the trip I was itchy, bloated and had a massive stomachache. Beef jerky and Milk Duds were not my friend. Top that off with a corn dog and two sixty-four ounce caffeinated sodas and I was a clusterfuck waiting to happen.

Thank the Goddess that New England was gorgeous in the fall. The colors were breathtaking, but they did little to calm my indigestion. The Kia had no radio reception, but luckily it did come with a country compilation CD that was stuck in the CD player. I was going deaf from the heartfelt warblings about pickup trucks, back roads and barefoot red necks—pretending to be mortal sucked. Six more hours and twenty-one minutes to go—shit.

"I can do this. I have to do this. I will do this," I shouted at the alarmed driver of a minivan while stopped at a traffic light in Bumfuck, Idon'tknowwhere.

"I'm baaaaaaack," something hissed from behind me.

"What the fu...?" I shrieked and jerked the wheel to the right, avoiding a bus stop and landing the car in a shallow ditch. "Who said that?"

"I diiiiiiiid," the ominous voice whispered. "Have yuoooooo missssssssed me?"

"Um, sure," I mumbled as I quietly removed my seatbelt and prepared to dive out of the car and try and catch a lift with the woman I'd terrified in the minivan. "I've missed you a ton."

"You look like shiiiiiiit in ooooorrrrangeeeee," it informed me.

That stopped me. Whatever monster or demon was in the backseat had just gone one step too far.

Scare me? Fine.

Insult me? Fry.

"Excuse me?" I snapped and whipped around to smite the fucker. Where was he? Was he invisible? "Show yourself."

"Down heeeeere on the floooooor," the thing said.

Peering over the seat, I gagged and threw up in my mouth just a little. This could not be happening. I pinched myself hard and yelped from the pain. It *was* happening and it was probably going to get ugly in twelve seconds.

"Um, hi Fabio, long time no see," I choked out, wondering if I made a run for it if he would follow and kill me. Or at the very least, would he get behind the wheel of the Kia and run me over...three times. "You're looking kind of alive."

"Thank youuuuuuuu," he said as he hopped over the seat and landed with a squishy thud entirely too close to me.

I plastered myself against the door and debated my next move. Fabio looked bad. He still resembled a cat, but he was kind of flat in the middle, his head was an odd shape and his tail cranked to the left. Most of his black fur still covered him except for a large patch on his face, which made him resemble a pinkish troll. He didn't seem too angry, but I did kill him. To be fair, I didn't mean to. I didn't know he was under the wheel and I kind of freaked and hit reverse and drive several times before I got out and screamed bloody murder. "So what are you doing here?"

"Not exxxxxxactly sure." He shook his little black semi-furred head and an ear fell off.

"Oh shit," I muttered and flicked it to the floor before he noticed. "I'm really sorry about killing you."

"No worrrrrries. I quite enjoyed being buried in a Prrrrraaada shoeeee box."

"I thought that was a nice touch," I agreed. "Did you notice I left the shoe bags in there as a blanket and pillow?"

"Yessssssssssssss. Very comfortable." He nodded and gave me a grin that made my stomach lurch.

"Alrighty then, the question of the hour is are you still dead or um..."

"I thiiiink I'm aliiiiive. As soon as I realliiiized I was breathing I loooooked for you."

"Wow." I was usually more eloquent, but nothing else came to mind.

"I have miiiiiiiised you, Zeeeeldaaaa."

Great, now I felt horrible. I killed him and he rose from the dead to find me because he missed me. I should take him in my arms and cuddle him, but I feared all the jerky and Duds would come flying from my mouth if I tried. He deserved better than me.

"Look, Fabio...I was a shitty witch for you. You should find a witch that will treat you right."

"But I looooooovvve you," he said quietly. His little one-eared head drooped and he began to sniffle pathetically.

"You shouldn't love me," I reasoned. "I'm selfish and I killed you, albeit accidentally, and I'm wearing orange."

"I can fix that," he offered meekly. "Would that make you looooooove meeeee?"

I felt nauseous and it wasn't from all the crap I'd shoved in my mouth while driving to meet my destiny. The little disgusting piece of fur had feelings for me. Feelings I didn't even come close to deserving or returning. And now to make matters worse, he was offering to magic me some clothes...If I said yes, it was a win-win. I'd get new clothes and he'd think I loved him. Asshats on fire, what in the hell was love anyway?

"Um...I would seem kind of shallow if I traded my love for clothes," I mumbled as I bit down on the inside of my cheek to keep from declaring my worthless love in exchange for non-orange attire.

"Well, youuuuuu are somewhat superficial, but that's not alllllllll your fault," Fabio said as he squished a little closer and placed the furry side of his head in my lap.

"Thank you, I think." A compliment was a compliment, no matter how insulting.

"You're most welcome," he purred. "How would you know what loooooove is? Your mother was a hoooooooker and your poor father was in the darrrrrk about your existence most of your liiiiiiiife."

"My mother was loose," I admitted, "but she did the best she could. However, my father, whoever the motherfuck he is, just took off after he knocked up my mom. And P.S.—I'm the only one allowed to call my mom a hooker. As nice as the fable was you told me about my dad...it's bullshit."

"Noooooooo, actually it's not," Fabio said as he lifted his piercing green eyes to mine.

"Do you know the bastard?" I demanded, noticing for the first time how our eyes matched. That wasn't uncommon. Most familiars took on the traits of their witches, but I wished he hadn't taken on mine. It would make it much harder to pawn the thing off on someone else if he looked too much like me.

"I knoooooow of him."

"So where the hell is he if he knows about me now?" My eyes narrowed dangerously and blue sparks began to cover my arms.

Fabio quickly backed away in fear of getting crispy. "Asssssssssss the story goes, a spell was cast on him by your mooooooother when he learned of your existence. From what I've heard he's been trying to break the spelllllllllll by doing penance."

I rolled my eyes and laughed. "How's that working out for the assmonkey?"

"Apparently not veeeeeeery well if he hasn't shown himself yet."

I considered Fabio's fairytale and wished for a brief moment it was true. Maybe my father didn't know about me. I always thought he didn't want me. That's what my mom had said. Of course she was certifiable and I'd left her house the moment I'd turned eighteen, but I did love her in the same way a dog still loved the owner who kicked them.

Fabio's story was utter crap, but it was sweet that he cared. Other than Winnie and Baba Yopaininmyass, not many did.

"Where did you learn all that fiction?" I asked as I eased the lime green piece of dog poo back onto the road before the police showed up and mistook me for an escaped convict.

"Yourrrrrrrr file," he answered as he dug his claws into the strap of the seat belt and pulled it across his mangled body. "Evvvvvvvery familiar gets a file on their witch."

"Here, let me," I said as I pulled the strap and clicked it into the lock. "Was there anything else interesting in my file?" The damn cat knew more about me than I did.

"Nothing I caaaaaan share."

I pursed my lips so I wouldn't swear at him—hard but doable. I wanted info and I knew how to get it. "What if I reattached your ear? Would you tell me one thing you're not supposed to?" I bargained.

"I'mmmmm missssssssing an ear?" he shrieked, aghast.

"Yep, I flicked it under the seat so you wouldn't flip."

His breathing became erratic and I worried he would heave a hairball or something worse. "Yesssssss, reattach it, please."

I opened my senses, and let whatever magic Baba Yasshole had let me keep, flow through me. Light purple healing flames covered my arms, neck and face. Fabio's ear floated up from under the passenger seat and drifted to his head. As it connected back, I had a thought. It was selfish and not...

"Hey Fab, do you mind if I fill in the fur on your face?" It would be so much easier to look at the little bastard if I didn't see raw cat skin.

"Ohhhhhhhhhh my, I'm missing fur?" He was positively despondent. Clearly he hadn't looked in a mirror since his resurrection.

"Um, it's just a little," I lied. "I can fix it up in a jiff."

"Thhhhhhank you, that would be loooovely."

The magic swirled through me. It felt so good. The pokey had blocked Winnie and I from using magic and I'd missed it terribly. The silky warm purple mist skimmed over Fabio's body and the hair reappeared. Without his permission I unflattened his midsection, reshaped his head and uncranked his tail. It was the least I could do since I'd caused it in the first place.

"There. All better," I told him and glanced over to admire my handiwork. He looked a lot better. He was still a bit mangy, but that was how he'd always been. At least he no longer looked like living road kill. "Your turn."

"Your Aunt Hildy was your father's sisssssssster and she wasssss freakin' crazy," he hissed with disgust.

"You knew her?"

"Ahh no, but sheeeeeee was legendary," he explained.

"Why the hell did she leave me her house?" I asked, hoping for some more info. I'd already assumed she was my deadbeat dad's sister. I wanted something new.

"I suppose you will take ooooover for her," Fabio informed me as he lifted and extended his leg so he could lick his balls.

"Get your mouth off your crotch while we're having a conversation," I snapped.

"Youuuuu would do it if youuuuuu could," he said.

"Probably," I muttered as I zoomed past six cars driving too slow for my mood. "But since I can't, you're not allowed to either."

"Can I dooooooo it in private?" he asked.

"Um, sure. Now tell me what crazy old Aunt Hildy did for a living so I know what I'm getting into here."

"No clue," Fabio said far too quickly.

"You know, I could run your feline ass over again," I threatened.

"Yeeeeeep, but I have six lives left."

"That's just fucking great."

Chapter Three

"What the fu...? I'm naked," I screamed somewhere around mile marker thirtytwowhatthehell in Pennsylvania. "What are you doing?"

"Trying to give youuuu a new outfiiiiit," Fabio whined as he turned away in horror.

I was unsure if I was more pissed that I was naked in the driver's seat of a lime green Kia or the fact that he clearly found me heinous to look at.

"You know," I ground out through clenched teeth, "most people consider me hot."

"Yessssssss, well, I'm a cat and I find yoooooour nudity allllaaaarming."

"Then dress me," I snapped. "In something really cute and expensive to make up for insulting my exposed knockers."

"Your knockers are looooovely, but it's not apppppppropriate for me to ogle your undraaaaaped body." He was a freakin' wreck.

"Is that against some kind of witch/familiar law?" I demanded as I looked down at myself. I looked good. Witches had crazy fast metabolisms and all of us were stupidly pretty.

"Yessssssss," he said as he twitched uncomfortably in his seat.

"Naked here," I reminded him.

The car filled with magic so quickly I gasped and held on to the steering wheel with all my might. The little fucker was strong. Who knew he had so much magic stored up in his mangy little carcass? A heat covered my body and I swerved to miss a semi truck.

"For the love of the Goddess," I shouted. "Hurry up or we're going to die here."

"Do youuuu want paaaaants or a skirt?" he asked.

"At the moment I'm not picky. I'm panicked. Just make sure it's not orange and I'll be happy."

"Asssssss youuuu wish."

The magic receded as quickly as it had begun. I was too shaken to even look down to see if I was dressed. I was getting rid of him as soon as I could. He was a fucking menace—not that I was a prize—but an imbalanced cat was more insanity than even I could handle.

"Dooooo you liiiike it?" he asked with an absurd amount of pride in his voice.

"I'll tell you in an hour when I get up the courage to look down. Where in the hell did you get so much magic? Familiars are not supposed to be stronger than their witches."

"I'm nooooot stronger," he insisted. "Youuuuu are stronger thaaaaan you know."

"Well, at the moment I'm not. Boobah Yumpa has me running on half a tank," I told him. "It's part of my punishment for killing you."

"Buuuuut I'm not deeeeead," he replied logically.

He was correct, but Butthole Yaga never changed her mind. Ever. It was actually something I liked about her, though I would never tell her. I'd grown up so horrendously, any female authority figure who had semi-sane rules was appealing to me.

"Yeah, she doesn't cave easily."

"You're wearing Maaaaax Midnight jeans and a vintage Minnie Mouuuuuse t-shirt with hot piiiink combat boots," he said.

That gave me pause. Hot pink combat boots were beyond awesome and Max Midnight jeans cost seven hundred dollars a pop. My freakin' cat had good taste. Maybe I'd keep him a little while longer.

"Are you serious?"

"Yessssss. I can change you iiiiif that diiispleases you."

"NO," I shouted. I wasn't sure if we would live through another change, plus if what he said was true I was a very happy camper. I glanced down and sighed with joy and relief. He was true to his word and I looked hot. "I like it."

His purr was cute until I looked over at him and noticed he was going for his nut sack again. "What did I tell you about that?" I glared at him in disgust.

"Soooooorrry," he whispered contritely. "Habit."

"Well Fabio, you're going to have to break that one or I'll get you neutered."

139

"Youuuuuuu wouldn't." He gasped and crossed his little kitty legs over his jewels.

"Try me."

That shut him up for about five minutes and seven seconds.

"Are weeeeeeee there yet?"

"No."

"How much looooooonger?"

"I don't know."

"More thaaaaaan two hours?"

"No clue."

"More than three hoooooouuuuurs?"

I bit down on my bottom lip so I didn't shout a spell at him that would permanently destroy his voice box. I was certain that wouldn't go over well with Booboo Yoogu.

"Willlllllll it be soooooon?"

"Fabio?"

"Yesssssss, Zelda?"

"Lick your balls."

"Reallllllllly?" He was so excited I cringed.

"Yes really, but get in the back seat. However, if I hear any slurping or purring I will throw your furry ass out of the window and leave you there. Are we clear?"

"Duuuuuly noted."

He jumped in the back seat and we had a peaceful ride the rest of the way there.

***

Aunt Hildy's house sat high on a hill and was the most beautiful thing I'd ever seen. It was a white Victorian with a wraparound porch and turrets. Wild flowers covered the grounds and the trees blazed with color. A few major drawbacks kept me from screaming with joy at my good fortune. It was located in the middle of nowhere. Since we had little to no supplies we trekked to town. The closest town, if you could call it that, was a half an hour away and consisted of Main Street. The town square was dominated by a statue of a cement bear missing one side of his head. The rest of the block included a barbershop, hardware store, gas station and a mom and pop grocery. Awesome.

We made a quick stop at the gas station and I gassed up the Kia with a credit card, *probably stolen*, that Fabio happened to have and then went to the grocery. I winced at the rotting fruit and vegetables and headed for the frozen and canned aisles. Ten frozen pizzas, two tubs of ice cream, and fifteen cans of brand-less spaghetti later I got in line at the checkout behind the hottest guy I'd ever seen. What in the hell was the Goddess's gift to women doing in Buttcrack, West Virginia? Maybe this place wasn't so bad...

His ass in his jeans was enough to make my mouth water and he smelled like heaven. Nine months in the magic pokey were enough to make any girl horny, but this guy was something else. I made a couple of girly sounds hoping to get his attention, but failed—so I touched his butt. Not grabbed—kind of brush-touched accidently on purpose.

"You could have asked first," a deep sexy voice informed me without even turning around.

"I'm sorry," I said politely to his back. "I have no idea what you're talking about."

"You could have requested to cop a feel of my ass." He turned around and I almost dropped to the floor. He wasn't just pretty, he was redonkulous gorgeous. Dark wavy hair, blue eyes, lashes that belonged on a girl, a body to die for and a face that would make the Angels weep. Oh. My. Hell.

"It was in my way. Consider yourself lucky. I almost slapped it."

His laugh went all the way to my woowoo and I was certain I crushed the can of Spaghettios I was clutching.

"Well, beautiful girl," he drawled in a Southern accent that made my brain short out, "I'd suggest you watch your ass. If it gets in my way I'll do much more than slap it."

"Promise?" I challenged.

He considered me for a long moment and then winked. "Promise."

I held on to the counter as I watched him walk out of the store and realized I didn't even know his name.

Whatever. I didn't need to get into any messy relationship. Hell, I'd never maintained a relationship in my life. I'd always had lots of boyfriends, but the minute it got serious I was out of there. Fast. Plus, I rarely dated mortals. Mr. Fine Ass didn't really look like relationship material. However, he did look like awesome one or two or three night stand material... Crap. I supposed I'd have to grocery shop on a regular basis. I grabbed my bags and went back to my new reality.

"Diiiiid you get my pasta?" Fabio inquired. He'd moved back to the front seat as he was clearly done attending to his gonads.

"Yep."

"Annnnd fresh tomatoes, baaaaasil and garlic?"

"Yep." He'd find out soon enough he was going to be eating Spaghettios. That was the price he'd have to pay for cleaning his Johnson for three hours, plus the fresh stuff would have killed him more certainly than my car had. "You ready to check out our new digs?"

"Asssss ready as I'll ever beeeeeee," he said with disgust.

"I'm not really buying that you didn't know Hildy," I said dryly. "You seem to be having an awful lot of issues here."

"It's heeeeer reputation," he shot back. "I don't liiiike this."

"Well buddy, neither do I, but if I don't figure out why I'm here Buttcrack Yoogiemamma will turn me into a mortal on Halloween. So we're going to the house and we are going to fucking like it. You got it?"

"Yesssssss," he answered morosely. "Gooot it."

Excerpt from

Fashionably Dead

Prologue

I drew hard on the cigarette and narrowed my eyes at the landscape before me. Graves, tombstones, crypts . . . she didn't belong here. Hell, I didn't belong here. My eyes were dry. I'd cried so much there was nothing left. I exhaled and watched as the blue grey smoke wafted out over the plastic flowers decorating the headstones.

Five minutes. I just needed five minutes and then I could go back . . .

"That's really gross," Gemma said, as she rounded the corner of the mausoleum I was hiding behind and scared the hell out of me. She fanned the smoke away and eyed me. "She wanted you to quit, maybe now would be a good time."

"Agreed. It's totally gross and disgusting and I'm going to quit, regardless of the fact that other than you, Marlboro Lights are my best friend . . . but today is definitely not the day," I sighed and took another long drag.

"That's pathetic," she chuckled.

"Correct. Do you have perfume and gum?"

"Yep." She dug through her purse and handed me a delicate bottle.

"I can't use this. It's the expensive French shit."

"Go for it," she grinned. "You're gonna need it. You smell like an ashtray and your mother is inside scaring people to death."

"Son of a . . . " I moaned and quickly spritzed myself. "I thought she left. She didn't want to come in the first place."

"Could have fooled me," Gemma said sarcastically, handing over a piece of gum and shoving me from my hiding place.

"Come on," I muttered, as my bossy best friend pushed me back to my beloved grandmother's funeral.

***

The hall was filled with people. Foldout tables lined the walls and groaned under the weight of casseroles, cakes and cookies. Men and women, most of whom I knew, milled around and ate while they gossiped. Southern funerals were a time to socialize and eat. A lot.

As I made my way through the crowd and accepted condolences, I got an earful of information I could have happily lived without. I learned that Donna Madden was cheating on her husband Greg, Candy Pucker had gained thirty pounds from eating Girl Scout cookies and had shoved her fat ass into a heinous sequined gown, *for the funeral no less,* and Sam Boomaster, the Mayor, was now a homosexual. Hell, I just wanted to leave, but I had to find my mother before she did something awful.

"I loved her." Charlie stopped me in my tracks and grabbed my hand in his old gnarled one.

His toupee was angled to the left and his black socks and sandals peeked out from his high-water plaid pants. He was beautiful.

"Me too," I smiled.

"You know I tried to court her back in the day, but she only had eyes for your Grandpa." He smoothed his sweater vest and laid a wet one on my cheek . . . and if I'm not mistaken, *and I'm not,* he grabbed my ass.

"Charlie, if you touch my butt again, I'll remove your hand." I grinned and adjusted his toupee. He was a regular in the art class I taught at the senior center and his wandering hands were infamous.

"Can't blame a guy for trying. You have a nice ass there, Astrid! You look like one of them there supermodels! Gonna make some lucky man very happy one day," he explained seriously.

"With my ass?"

"Well now, your bosom is nothing to scoff at either and your legs . . . " he started.

"Charlie, I'm gonna cut you off before you wax poetic about things that will get you arrested for indecency."

"Good thinking, girlie!" he laughed. "If you ever want to hear stories about your Nana from when we were young, I'd be happy to share."

"Thanks, Charlie, I'd like that."

I gave him a squeeze, holding his hands firmly to his sides and made my way back into the fray.

As I scanned the crowd for my mother, my stomach clenched. After everything I had to put up with today, the evil approaching was just too much. Martha and Jane, the ancient matriarchs of the town and the nastiest gossips that ever lived were headed straight for me. Fuck.

"I suppose you'll get an inheritance," Jane snapped as she looked me up and down. "You'll run through it like water."

"Your Nana, God bless her, was blind as a bat when it came to you," Martha added caustically. "I mean, my God, what are you? Thirty and unmarried? It's just downright disrespectable."

"I'm twenty-nine, happily single and getting it on a regular basis," I said, enjoying the way their thin lips hung open in an impressive O.

"Well, I've never," Jane gasped.

"Clearly. You should try it sometime. I understand Mr. Smith is so vision impaired, you might have a shot there."

Their appalled shrieks were music to my ears and I quickly made my escape. Nana would have been a bit disappointed with my behavior, but she was gone.

Time to find the reason I came back in here for . . . I smelled her before I saw her. A waft of Chanel perfume made the lead ball in my stomach grow heavier. I took a deep breath, straightened my very vintage Prada sheath that I paid too much for, plastered a smile on my face, said a quick prayer and went in to the battle.

"Mother, is everything alright?"

She stood there mutely and stared. She was dressed to the nines. She didn't belong here . . . in this town, in this state, in my life.

"I'm sorry, are you speaking to me?" she asked. Shit, she was perfect . . . on the outside. Gorgeous and put together to a degree I didn't even aspire to. On the inside she was a snake.

"Um, yes. I asked you if . . . " I stammered.

"I heard you," she countered smoothly. "If you can't bother to comply with my wishes, I can't be bothered to answer you."

"Right," I muttered and wished the floor would open and swallow me. "I'm sorry, I meant Petra. Petra, is everything alright?"

"No, everything is not alright," she hissed. "I have a plane to catch and I have no more time or patience to make chit chat with backward rednecks. It was wrong of you to ask me to be here."

"Your mother died," I said flatly. "This is her funeral and these people are here to pay their respects."

"Oh for God's sake, she was old and lived well past her time."

I was speechless. Rare for me, but if anyone was capable of shocking me to silence, it was my mother.

"So, like I said, I have a plane to catch. I'll be back next week." She eyed me critically, grimacing at what she saw. "You need some lipstick. You're lucky you got blessed with good genes because you certainly don't do anything to help."

With that loving little nugget, she turned on her stiletto heel and left. I glanced around to see if we'd been overheard and was mortified to see we had clearly been the center of attention.

"Jesus, she's mean," Gemma said, pulling me away from prying eyes and big ears.

"Do I look awful?" I whispered, feeling the heat crawl up my neck as the mourners looked on with pity. Not for my loss, but for my parentage.

"You're beautiful," Gemma said. "Inside and out."

"I need to smoke," I mumbled. "Can we leave yet?"

Gemma checked her watch. "Yep, we're out of here."

"I don't want to go home yet," I said, looking around for Bobby Joe Gimble, the funeral director. Where in the hell was he and did I need to tip him? Shit, I had no clue what funeral etiquette was. "Do I have to . . . ?"

"Already took care of everything," Gemma told me. "Let's go."

"Where to?" I asked. Damn, I was grateful she was mine.

"Hattie's."

"Thank you, Jesus."

***

Hattie's sold one thing and one thing only. Ice cream. Homemade, full of fat, heart attack inducing ice cream. It was probably my favorite place in the world.

"I'll have a triple black raspberry chip in a cone cup," I said as I eyed all the flavors. I didn't know why I even looked at them. I was totally loyal to my black raspberry chip. My ice cream couldn't talk back to me, break up with me or make me feel bad. Of course, my love could extend the size of my ass, but I wasn't even remotely concerned about that today. Besides, I planned a very long run for later. I needed to clear my head and be alone.

"Sorry about your loss, Sugar," Hattie said and I nodded. Her big fleshy arms wobbled as she scooped out my treat. "Do you want sprinkles and whipped cream on that, Baby?"

"Um . . . " I glanced over at Gemma who grinned and gave me a thumbs up. "Yes, yes I do."

"Me too," Gemma added, "but I want mint chip, please."

"You got it, Sugar Buns," Hattie said and handed me a monstrous amount of ice cream. "It's on me today, Astrid. I feel just terrible I couldn't be at the funeral."

"That's okay, Hattie. You and Nana were such good friends. I want your memories to be of that."

"Thank you for that, Darlin'. Ever since my Earl died from siphoning gasoline, I haven't been able to set foot near that goddamn funeral parlor."

I swallowed hard. Her late ex-husband Earl had siphoned gasoline since he was ten. His family owned the local gas station and apparently, as legend had it, he enjoyed the taste. But on the fateful day in question, he'd been smoking a cigar while he did it . . . and blew himself to kingdom come. It was U-G-L-Y. Earl was spread all over town. Literally. He and Hattie had been divorced for years and hated each other. It was no secret he had fornicated with over half the older women in town, but when he died like that, he became a saint in her eyes.

I bit down on the inside of my cheek. Hard. Although it was beyond inappropriate, whenever anyone talked about Earl, I laughed.

"Astrid totally understands." Gemma gave Hattie a quick hug and pushed me away from the counter before I said or did something unforgivable.

"Thanks," I whispered. "That would have been bad."

"Yep," Gemma grinned and shoveled a huge spoon of ice cream in her mouth.

"Where in the hell do you put that?" I marveled at her appetite. "You're tiny."

"You're a fine one to talk, Miss I Have the World's Fastest Metabolism."

"That's the only good thing I inherited from the witch who spawned me," I said and dug in to my drug of choice. I winced in pain as my frozen ice cream ass-extender went straight to the middle of my forehead.

"Are you okay?" Gemma asked.

I took a deep breath and pinched the bridge of my nose. God, I hated brain freezes. "No, not right now, but I've decided to change some stuff. Nana would want me to."

My best friend watched me silently over her ice cream.

"I'm going to stop smoking, get a real career, work out every day, date someone who has a job and not a parole officer, get married, have two point five kids and prove that I was adopted."

"That's a pretty tall order. How are you gonna make all that happen?" she asked, handing me a napkin. "Wipe your mouth."

"Thanks," I muttered. "I have no fucking idea, but I will succeed . . . or die trying."

"Good luck with that."

"Um, thanks. Do you mind if we leave here so I can chain smoke 'til I throw up so it will be easier to quit?"

"Is that the method you're going to use?" Gemma asked, scooping up our unfinished ice cream and tossing it.

"I know it seems a little unorthodox, but I read it worked for Jennifer Aniston."

"Really?"

"No, but it sounded good," I said, dragging her out of Hattie's.

"God, Astrid," Gemma groaned. "Whatever you need to do I'm here for you, but you have to quit. I don't want you to die. Ever."

"Everybody dies," I said quietly, reminded that the woman I loved most had died only a week ago. "But I've got too fucking much to do to die any time soon."

Chapter 1

"There are ten thousand ways to express yourself creatively," I huffed, yanking on my running shoes. "My God, there's acting, painting, sewing, belly dancing, cooking . . . Shit, scrapbooking is creative." I shoved my arms into my high school sweatshirt that had seen better days.

"You're not actually wearing that," Gemma said, helping herself to my doughnut.

"Yep, I actually am." I grabbed my breakfast out of her hand and shoved it in my mouth. "And by the way, I've decided to be a movie star."

"But you can't act," my best friend reminded me.

"That's completely beside the point," I explained, taking the sweatshirt off. I hated it when Gemma was right. "Half the people in Hollywood can't act."

"Don't you think it might be wise to choose a career that you actually have the skills to do?"

"Nope, I told you I'm making changes. Big ones."

I bent over and tied my running shoes. Maybe if I just ran forever, I would stop hurting. Maybe if I found something meaningful, I could figure out who in the hell I was.

Gemma picked up my soda and took a huge swig. "You're an artist and a damn good one. You should do something with that."

"Yeah, maybe," I said, admiring my reflection in the microwave. Holy hell, my hair was sticking up all over my head. "Why didn't you tell me my hair exploded?"

"Because it's funny," Gemma laughed.

"I'll never make it in show business if people see my hair like this," I muttered and tried to smooth it down.

"Astrid, you will never make it in show business no matter what your hair looks like. You may be pretty, but you can't act your way out of a hole and you suck as a liar," Gemma informed me as she flopped down on my couch and grabbed the remote.

"Your confidence in me is overwhelming." I picked out a baseball cap and shoved it over my out of control curls. "If the movie star thing doesn't work out, I might open a restaurant."

"Did you become mentally challenged during the night at some point?" she asked as she channel surfed faster than any guy I ever dated.

"Gimme that thing." I yanked the remote away from her. "What in the hell are you trying to find?"

"*Jersey Shore*."

"For real?" I laughed.

"For real for real," she grinned.

"Don't you have a home?" I asked.

"Yep. I just like yours better."

I threw the remote back at her and grabbed my purse. If I was going to be a famous actress, or at the very least a chef, I needed to get started. But before I could focus on my new career, I had business to take care of. Very important business . . .

"Where are you going?" Gemma yawned. "It's 8:00 on a Sunday morning."

"I'm going running," I said, staring at the ceiling.

"Oh my God," Gemma grinned, calling me out on my lie. "Astrid, since when do you run with your purse?"

"Okay fine," I snapped. "I'm going to run a few errands and say goodbye forever to one of my best friends today."

Gemma gaped at me. Her mouth hung open like she'd had an overdose of Novocain at the dentist. "So today is the day? You really going to end it?"

"I don't really have a choice, since there's so much damn money riding on it."

"Oh my God," she squealed and punched me in the arm. "I'm so proud of you."

"Don't be proud yet," I muttered, praying I'd be successful with my breakup plans.

"You didn't have to take the bet," Gemma said.

"Yes, I did," I said and shook my head with disgust. "Nothing else has worked. Voodoo has to."

"Voodoo?"

"Yep."

"Good luck with that."

"Thanks," I said as I slapped on some lip gloss. "I'm gonna need it."

"Yes, you are," Gemma grinned. "Yes, you are."

***

It was hot and I was sweaty and I wondered for the umpteenth time if I was losing my mind. I needed to stop making bets that were impossible to win. Maybe I could be a social smoker or I could just hide it from everyone. I could carry perfume and gum and lotion and drive to the next town when I needed a nicotine fix.

"Excuse me, are you here to be hypnotized?" a feminine voice purred.

I glanced up from my spot on the filthy sidewalk and there stood the most beautiful woman I'd ever seen. I quickly stubbed out my cigarette, turned my head away in embarrassment and blew my smoke out. Reason number three hundred and forty-six to quit . . . impersonating a low class loser.

She looked foreign—Slavic or Russian. Huge violet-blue eyes, full lips, high cheekbones set in a perfect heart-shaped face, framed by tons of honey-gold blonde hair. Absolutely ridiculous. I felt a little inadequate. Not only was the face perfect, but the body was to die for. Long legs, pert boobies, ass-o-rific back side and about six feet tall. I was tall at 5 feet 9 inches, but she was *tall*.

"Well, I was," I explained, straightening up and trying to look less like a crumpled homeless mess from my seat on the sidewalk, "but they must have moved." I pointed to a rusted-out doorway.

"Oh no," the gorgeous Amazon giggled. Seriously, did she just giggle? "That's not the door. It's right over here." She grabbed my hand, her grip was firm and cool, and guided me to the correct door. A zap of electricity shot up my arm when she touched me. I tried to nonchalantly disengage my hand from hers, but she held mine fast. "Here we go." She escorted me into the lobby of a very attractive office.

"I don't know how I missed this," I muttered as she briskly led me to a very nice exam room. She released my

153

hand. Did that zap really just happen? Maybe I was already in nicotine withdrawal.

"Please have a seat." The blue eyed bombshell indicated a very soft and cozy looking pale green recliner.

"I'm sorry, are you the hypnotist?" I asked as I sat. Something didn't feel quite right. What was a gorgeous, Amazon Russian-looking chick doing in Mossy Creek, Kentucky? This was a tiny town, surely I would have seen her before.

"Yes, yes I am," she replied, sitting on a stool next to my comfy chair with an official-looking clipboard in her hand. "So you're here because . . . ?"

"Because . . . um, I want to stop smoking," I told her and then quickly added, "Oh, and I don't want to gain any weight." If you don't ask for the impossible, there's no way you'll ever get it.

Miss Universe very slowly and somewhat clinically looked me over from head to toe. "Your weight looks perfect. You are a very beautiful young woman. Are you happy with your body right now?"

"Yes," I replied slowly. Was she hitting on me? I didn't think so, but . . .

"That's good," she smiled. "I can guarantee that you will never gain weight again after you're hypnotized."

"Really?" I gasped. My God, that was incredible. Smoke free and at a weight I liked. This was the best day ever.

"Really," she laughed. "Now let's get started."

"Wait, don't I need to fill out a bunch of forms and pay and sign my life away in case you accidentally kill me or something?"

Blondie laughed so hard I thought she might choke. "No, no," she assured me and quickly pulled herself together. "My receptionist is at lunch . . . we'll take care of it afterwards. Besides, I've never killed anyone by accident."

"Ooookay." She was a little weird, but I supposed people with her occupation would be. She did guarantee me I would be smoke free and skinny. That did not suck. Wait . . . I needed to think this through. I was feeling unsettled and wary. She was odd, made me uncomfortable and had electric hands. On the flip side, she was very pretty, had a really nice office and promised no weight gain. Damn.

Would common sense or vanity prevail? And the winner is . . . vanity. By a landslide.

She leaned into me, her green eyes intense. I could have sworn her eyes were purple-y bluish. I was getting so tired. I prayed I wouldn't drool when I was out.

"Astrid, you need to clear your mind and look into my eyes," Miss Russia whispered.

"How do you know my name?" I mumbled. "I didn't tell you my name." Alarm bells went off in my brain. My pea-brain that never should have thought it was a good idea to get hypnotized at a strip mall on the bad side of town. You'd think a business called 'House of Hypnotism' might have tipped me off. Crap. These were not the decisions a smart and responsible, if not somewhat directionless, twenty-nine year old woman should make. I should have listened to my gut and gone with common sense.

The room started spinning. It felt like a carnival from hell. Blondie's mouth was so strange. There was something very unattractive going on with her mouth. It got kind of blurry, but it looked like . . . wait . . . maybe she was British. They all have bad teeth.

"I fink ooo shud stooop," I said, mangling the English language. I tried again. "Oow do ooo know my name?" When did I put marbles in my mouth? Who in the hell dimmed the lights and cranked the air conditioner?

"Oh Astrid, not only do I know your name," she smiled, her green eyes blazing, "I know everything about you, dear."

Chapter 2

I opened my eyes and immediately shut them. What in the hell time was it? What in the hell day was it? I snuggled deeper into my warm and cozy comforter and tried to go back to sleep. Why couldn't I go back to sleep? Something was wrong . . . very wrong. I just had no idea what it was.

Ignoring the panic that was bubbling to the surface, I leaned over the side of my bed and grabbed my purse. It was Prada. I loved Prada. I proudly considered myself a Prada whore, *albeit one who couldn't afford it.*

Everything seemed to be in there . . . wallet, phone, makeup, gum, under-used day planner. Nothing important was missing. I was being paranoid. Everything was fine.

I eyed my beloved out of season Prada sandals lying on my bedroom floor. Shoes always made me feel better. Only in New York or Los Angeles would anyone know my adored footwear was four seasons ago. Certainly not in Istillwearmyhairinamullet, Kentucky. I got them on sale. I paid six hundred dollars that I didn't have for them, but that was a deal considering they were worth a solid twelve hundred.

I pressed my fingers to the bridge of my nose and tried to figure out what day of the week it was. Good God, I had no clue. I suppose exhaustion had finally caught up with me, but I couldn't for the life of me remember what I had done to be so tired. I vaguely remembered driving home from somewhere. I glanced again at my awesome shoes, but even my beautiful sandals couldn't erase the sense of dread in the pit of my stomach.

"Focus on something positive," I muttered as I wracked my brain and snuggled deeper into my covers.

Shoes. Think about shoes . . . not the irrational suffocating fear that was making me itch. Bargains! That was it, I'd think about bargains. I loved getting a good bargain almost as much as I loved Prada. Unfortunately, I also had a huge love for cigarettes, and I needed to love one now. Right now. I rummaged through my purse and searched for a pack. Bingo! I found my own personal brand of heroin and lit up.

WTF? It wouldn't light because I couldn't inhale. Why couldn't I inhale? Was I sick? I felt my head; definitely no fever. My forehead felt like ice.

Okay, if at first you don't succeed . . . blah blah blah. I tried again. I couldn't inhale. Not only could I not inhale, I also couldn't exhale. Which would lead me to surmise I wasn't breathing. The panic I was avoiding had arrived.

"Fuck shit fuck fuck, this is a side effect. That's right, a side effect. A side effect of what?" I demanded to no one in particular since I was alone in my room. I knew it was something. It was on the tip of my brain . . . side effect . . . side effect of not smoking. Side effect of not smoking? What the hell does that even mean? For God's sake, why can't I figure this out? I have an I.Q. of 150, not that I put it to very good use.

"Wait," I hissed. "It's a side effect of the hypnotism."

God, that was bizarre, but that had to be it. I made that stupid bet with Gemma and got hypnotized to stop smoking by that big blonde Amazon at the House of Hypnotism. That's what I drove home from. I wasn't crazy. The Amazon must have forgotten to inform me that I wouldn't be able to breathe for awhile afterwards. That's what you get when you don't read the fine print. Did I even pay her? I'm sure I'll start breathing any second now. I'm so glad I figured this out. I feel better. For a minute there I thought I was dead.

I glanced out of my bedroom window at the full moon.

"Full moon? Oh my God, have I been in bed all day?"

I threw the covers off and stood quickly, still trying to figure out what day it was. The room spun violently and a wave of dizziness knocked me right back down on my ass. Little snippets of my dreams raced through my mind as I waited for the vertigo to pass.

God, that was a freaky dream. Oprah and Vampyres and yummy, creamy chocolate blood . . . you couldn't make that stuff up.

The room quit spinning and I stood up slowly, firmly grasping one of the posts of my beautiful four poster bed. I reached up high above my head, arched back and popped my sternum. Slightly gross, but it felt great. I ran my hands through my hair, rubbed the sleep out of my eyes and bit through my bottom lip. Mmm . . . crunchberries. I licked the tasty blood from my mouth.

I wondered what time it was. If it wasn't too late, I could get a run in and then I could . . . *bite through my bottom lip?? Crunchberries? What the fu . . . ?*

In my frazzled mental state, I heard a noise in the hallway outside my bedroom. I immediately dropped to a defensive squat on the floor. Way back in high school they told us, if you hear an intruder, get low . . . or was that for a fire? Shit, that was get low for a fire . . . what in the hell do I do for a burglar?

Good God, I was in my bra and panties. The blue granny panties with the unfortunate hole in the crotch. Not a good look for fending off burglars. Not a good look ever. On my never ending list of things to do I needed to add *throw out all panties over seven years old.*

I remained low, just in case. I duck walked over to my closet and grabbed one of my many old cheerleading trophies out of a cardboard box so I could kill my intruder. It was plastic, but it was pointy. I'd been meaning to give them to my eight year old neighbor. Thank God I was a procrastinator. Wait a minute . . . As I death-gripped my trophy I was overwhelmed with the scent of rain and orchids and Pop Tarts and cotton candy.

What the hell?

It wasn't a dream. She was here? And apparently from the smell of it, she had a guest. I'd just cannibalized my own lip, my blood tasted like crunchberries, I could smell people in my house, I couldn't breathe, my skin felt icy, and I think I might be . . .

"Astrid, are you awake?" Gemma called from right outside my door interrupting my ridiculous train of thought.

Oh thank you, Jesus. "Yes." Was that my voice? It sounded deeper and raspier. And sexier?

"Get out here," Gemma yelled. "Get dressed and change that underwear . . . it's nasty."

"Gemma, I have to tell you something weird, but you have to believe me and you can't get mad," I said through my closed door, ignoring the insultingly accurate underwear comment.

"I think I already know," she said from the other side.

"It's not about my haircut."

"You got your hair cut without me?" Gemma was appalled.

Shit, I thought she knew about my hair. What did she know then? *Good God, what in the hell was wrong with my bra? The girls were spilling out of it. Were they bigger? Did my bra shrink?* "Gem, um . . . I swear I meant to tell you about my hair. It was spur of the moment. Mr. Bruce dragged me into the salon and the next thing I knew, he set my baseball cap on fire, cut my hair into long layers and put in some kick ass highlights."

"Fine, Astrid." Her voice got tinny and high. "Just don't be surprised if I go get a perm without you."

"You wouldn't."

"I might," she threatened.

"Gem," I begged, "with me or without me, Do. Not. Get. A. Perm. That's so 1980s."

"You're right," Gemma sighed, "I'd get a lobotomy before I'd get a perm. What do you need to tell me?"

I gathered myself. I realized I was about to sound like an idiot, but when had that ever stopped me? I closed my eyes and let her rip. "Um . . . after my haircut, I got hypnotized by a big blonde Amazon gal to stop smoking, and now I can't breathe. I think it must be a side effect, but it's freaking me out." Gemma was silent on the other side of my bedroom door.

"You can't breathe?"

"No." I couldn't tell if she believed me.

"Are you sure?"

"I think I would know if I couldn't breathe," I shouted.

"Do I owe you a thousand bucks?"

"I'm not sure yet."

At least I was honest. The entire reason I'd gotten hypnotized was because I'd bet Gemma a thousand dollars I could quit smoking. I knew she thought it was a no-brainer bet due to the sorry fact that this was my ninth attempt to quit in the last three months. Nicotine gum, cold turkey, weaning off and all those self-help books weren't doing it for me. I needed outside assistance. Short of having my lips sewn shut, I hadn't been successful at quitting. Hypnotism was a last resort because having my lips sewn shut was simply not an option.

"Where did you get hypnotized?" she quizzed.

"House of Hypnotism over by the Chinese restaurant that serves cat."

Gemma was speechless. I was getting more nervous with each passing second. "Do you have a pulse?" she asked.

"I'm sorry, what did you just ask me?"

"I said," Gemma yelled through the door, "do you have a pulse?"

"What kind of a stupid question is that? Of course I have a . . . " I checked for my pulse, then I checked again, then I checked again and then I checked one more time. "Um . . . no," I whispered.

"You sure?"

"Positive."

"What's your skin temp?"

"Really cold," I told her.

What in the hell was wrong with her? She was awfully calm about the whole thing. She was silent for what felt like an eternity. These questions were right up Gemma's alley. She loved all things weird, especially anything astrological or supernatural. I could tell she was thinking because she was humming 'Billie Jean'. Gemma, besides being a Prada whore who like me couldn't afford it, knew the lyrics to every Michael Jackson song ever recorded. She wore black for an entire year after he died. "I think I know what's going on." She began to hum 'Thriller'.

"What's wrong with me?" I shrieked.

"Come out here, Astrid."

"Wait Gemma . . . am I dead?"

"Kinda," she said with excitement. The same kind of excitement she exuded when she tried to convince me of Bigfoot's existence. "Just get dressed and get out here."

I quickly whipped on some overpriced jeans that made my butt look asstastic and put on the first shirt my fingers touched. I pulled on some hot pink sequined Converse and made my way out to my living room. That took about ten and a half steps because my house was the size of a postage stamp.

Gemma was standing by the window bouncing like a ball, so excited she was about to burst . . . and the Queen of Daytime Talk was sprawled on my couch reading my diary. Wait . . . what?

"Holy Jesus," I gasped. "You're Opr . . . "

"Don't say it," my idol cut me off, throwing my diary aside as if I wouldn't notice she'd been reading my most private and embarrassing thoughts. "I'm not her, never fuckin' have been, never fuckin' will be. If you call me that, I'll leave. Trust me, that would be very fuckin' bad for you."

"Oookay, you have quite a vocabulary." I smiled, wondering if Gemma thought this was as screwy as I did. She did seem a little freaked, but not nearly enough to merit the fact Oprah was here. "If you're not Opr . . . I mean that woman who you look exactly like, then you are . . . ?"

I peeked around my tiny living room and looked for cameras. This had to be for a show segment. Right? Gemma must be in on the whole thing with Oprah.

Was she going to redecorate my crappy house or give me a car or tell me something wonderful about my birth mother?

That was impossible. My birth mother was actually the woman who, for lack of a better word, raised me and there wasn't much wonderful about her. My Nana, may she rest in peace, was wonderful. Her daughter, my mother . . . not so much. Hopefully, Oprah was here to redecorate.

"You're a Vampyre and I'm your fuckin' Guardian Angel," I'm-Not-Oprah grunted.

Gemma squealed and clapped her hands like a two year old at Christmas. Apparently they'd become great friends already, possibly bonding over Bigfoot. The dizziness now combined with total paranoia overtook me as my knees buckled and I dropped to the ground like a sack of potatoes.

"Wow . . . so not what I was expecting to hear." My stomach was queasy. This was starting to make me tingle, and not in a good way. I'm-Not-Oprah had to go. "Well, golly gee, look at the time; I suppose you have a train to catch . . . to Crazytown," I informed her in a bizarre cheerleader voice that I had no control over. "So you'd better get going." *Vampyre my ass. I'm-Not-Oprah is cuckoo loco crazy.* I crawled over to my front door and opened it with shaking hands and body, letting Oprah know she had to leave.

I'm-Not Oprah had the gall to laugh, and I don't mean just a little giggle. I mean a huge gut-busting, knee-slapping guffaw. *God, I need a cigarette.* Oh but wait . . . *I DON'T SMOKE ANYMORE BECAUSE I CAN'T BREATHE.* I was completely screwed. There had to be a logical answer to this clusterfuck. I just needed to think it through.

Ignoring the unexplainable situation in my home, I curled into a ball by my front door and went back through what I could remember. First, I'd gotten my hair cut and colored because it looked like hell. Then I chain-smoked half a pack of cigarettes getting my nerve up to get hypnotized to quit. After almost vomiting from the sheer amount of nicotine in my system, I got hypnotized to stop smoking. Good thinking on my part. Next, the ridiculously attractive Amazon woman who hypnotized me was successful because I will never smoke again. Good thinking on her part.

However, it was also beginning to look like I would never breathe again. So technically I was dead. The lack of pulse and air intake could attest to this, but clearly I wasn't dead because I was curled up on the floor thinking somewhat coherently and Oprah was in my house . . . What in the hell was I talking about? None of this was possible. I was dreaming. That had to be it. I was dreaming. I pinched myself. Hard.

"Ouch . . . shit." Not dreaming.

I slowly stood up, determined to kick Her Oprahness out of my house. My whole body began to tremble as I locked eyes with the insane talk show host sitting on my couch. I couldn't believe I was standing here looking at Oprah, who says she's not, who's telling me I'm a Vampyre, which don't exist, and she's a Guardian Angel, which again . . . don't exist. Besides, if they did, they certainly wouldn't have a mouth like hers.

"Oh my God," I moaned as another bizarre wave of dizziness came over me. The room grew darker and smaller. I'm-Not-Oprah and Gemma started to get blurry and a burning began in my gut. Flames ripped through my stomach and violently shot into my arms, my legs, my neck and head. My insides were shredding. I was thirsty . . . so very thirsty. God, it hurt so much. I floated above myself as my body crumpled to the floor. The buzzing in my head was deafening. I tried to take a deep breath, but that went nowhere fast.

"I'm dying," I groaned.

Crapballs, did I have good underwear on? No! I still had on light blue grannies with a not on purpose hole in the crotch. Oh my God, I'm dying with bad underpants on. My mother will have a fit. I can hear her now, "*Well, with underpants like that, it's no wonder Astrid couldn't get a man. She kept buying all that Prada, but she should have invested in a couple of pairs of decent panties.*" This was not good.

The blazing inferno inside me consumed my whole body. It was excruciating. I wasn't sure how much more I could take. I vaguely saw Oprah coming for me.

"Kill me please," I begged. She laughed and scooped me up like a rag doll and shoved my face to her neck. God, she smelled good. "Argrah," I gurgled.

"Just shut the fuck up and drink," I'm-Not-Oprah growled.

It was delicious, like rich dark chocolate, so smooth, so warm, so yummy. What was this? The pain slowly subsided and I realized I was curled up in I'm-Not-Oprah's lap with my teeth embedded in her neck. She was rocking me like a baby.

I removed what I'm fairly sure were my fangs from Oprah's neck. "What am I doing?" I calmly asked.

She looked down at me and smiled. Holy cow she looked like Oprah. "Drinking."

163

"Drinking what?" I inquired politely.

"O negative," she replied.

"O negative what?" I screeched, jerking to an upright position on her very ample lap.

"O negative Angel blood, dumbass," she bellowed. She stood up and dumped me on the floor as she walked over to retrieve my diary.

"Oh my God, you're not joking." I was horrified.

"No, I certifuckingly am not."

Visit www.robynpeteman.com for purchase links

Connect with Robyn Peterman

WEBSITE
http://www.robynpeterman.com

EMAIL
robyn@robynpeterman.com

TWITTER
https://twitter.com/robynpeterman

FACEBOOK
http://www.facebook.com/pages/Robyn-
Peterman/418985661472374?ref=hl

CONTEMPORARY BOOK BLOG
http://robynpeterman.blogspot.com

PINTEREST
http://pinterest.com/robynpeterman/boards/

GOODREADS
http://www.goodreads.com/author/show/6545317.Roby
n_Peterman

Other Books by Robyn Peterman

HAND CUFFS AND HAPPILY EVER AFTERS

How Hard Can It Be?
Size Matters
Cop A Feel

and unfortunately
Pirate Dave and His Randy Adventure

(Career ending spoofy novella based on HHCIB)

HOT DAMNED SERIES

Fashionably Dead
Fashionably Dead Down Under
Hell on Heels

For more information about her books, visit
www.robynpeterman.com

About Robyn Peterman

Robyn Peterman writes because the people inside her head won't leave her alone until she gives them life on paper.

Her addictions include laughing really hard with friends, shoes (the expensive kind), Target, Coke Zero Cherry with extra ice in a Styrofoam cup, bejeweled reading glasses, her kids, her super-hot hubby and collecting stray animals.

A former professional actress with Broadway, film and T.V. credits, she now lives in the South with her family and too many animals to count.

Writing gives her peace and makes her whole, plus having a job where you can work in your underpants works really well for her. You can leave Robyn a message via the Contact Page and she'll get back to you as soon as her bizarre life permits! She loves to hear from her fans!

Visit **www.robynpeterman.com** for more information.

Made in the USA
Middletown, DE
27 December 2019

82082457R00096